"I HADN'T THOUGHT ABOUT DYING HERE. IT'S HARD TO GET READY FOR IT."

Raider came forward and took the weeping Genevieve in his arms. He stared at the walls of their cell and said, "I don't reckon anybody's ever ready."

Genevieve looked into his eyes. "Raider, once more before I die."

"Once more what?"

"You know what I mean," Genevieve replied. She backed away from him a step and calmly and deliberately unbuttoned her blouse....

J.D. HARDIN

GUNFIRE AT SPANISH ROCK

PLAYBOY
PAPERBACKS

Published simultaneously in the United States and Canada by Playboy Paperbacks, New York, New York. Printed in the United States of America. Library of Congress Catalog Card Number: 81-82968. First edition.

Books are available at quantity discounts for promotional and industrial use. For further information, write to Premium Sales, Playboy Paperbacks, 1633 Broadway, New York, New York 10019.

ISBN: 0-867-21002-8

First printing February 1982.

CHAPTER ONE

Raider, who had been silent for maybe the past hour, rode his claybank mare beside the medicine wagon, sometimes pulling ahead a little, sometimes dropping behind a few lengths, but, on the whole, matching the slower pace of the vehicle. Its iron-rimmed wheels bounced over the sunbaked ruts of the winding trail that was a road in name only, and on each side of its enclosed cab was the sign that said, in gaudy letters, DR. WEATHERBEE'S ME-DICINAL WONDERS.

Doc, on the wagon's seat, rested his thumbs lightly atop the reins but did little to manipulate them. Once he got his mule, Judith, pointed in the right direction, she pretty much kept going on her own. A mule, though stubborn, was smarter than a horse any day, Doc believed, though he knew Raider would give him an argument on that.

The New Mexico sun glared down on both men, imperturbable, relentless. The dry, scarred land, cut by centuries of erosion into mesas and arroyos, stretched away from them in all directions. Ahead, on the horizon, was a jagged blue line like the cutting edge of a flint arrowhead—an offshoot ridge of the Sangre de Cristo mountains.

"Hey, Rade," Doc finally said.

Raider turned his dark eyes toward his partner. "Yeah?"

"Why don't you sit here a spell?" Doc shifted slightly in the wagon seat.

Raider spat dryly. "Why'n hell should I?"

"To rest your ass." Doc's expression was solemn,

but there was a faint crinkling around his eyes to show that he was pirooting his taller, more taciturn companion.

"Might rest my ass, but it'd play hell with my cock," said Raider.

"Oh? How come?"

"Way that wagon jiggles and bounces. Gives you a hard-on every time. And what would I do with a hard-on way out here a hundred miles past nowhere?"

Doc laughed aloud. "I can see you've got your troubles. Well, cheer up. We'll be in Tesqua by tomorrow. Maybe you'll find relief there."

Raider nodded, making no attempt to match Doc's laugh, though Doc, long familiar with the onetime Arkansas farmer's reactions, knew he'd been mildly diverted by the exchange of words and the break in the hot, dry silence.

An unlikely pair, Raider and Doc Weatherbee, some might say: Raider with sweeping mustaches and a greasy buckskin jacket, Doc in his citified suit and pearl-gray derby. But in their differences they complemented each other, and maybe that was why they got along. There were times when Doc's college education came in handy. Same for Raider's down-to-earth way of seeing most things the way they really were.

Doc settled back as the wagon creaked and jostled along and tried to make his mind blank—which for him wasn't easy. But he had to sustain the boredom of the journey somehow, and he had to accept the fact that there were usually long, drawn-out journeys whenever he and Raider were sent on an assignment. Tesqua, this time—little town up the Brazos, after it branched off from the Rio Grande just above Santa Fe, nestling there, far west of Taos, almost up against the continental

divide. Doc had scarcely heard of the place before
Willy Pinkerton, in the Denver office of the Pinkerton National Detective Agency, had given them
the details of their mission and sent them—along
with the wagon and mule—on the train to Santa
Fe. His Scottish blood ever alert to expenses, he'd
tried to send only the two men, but they'd insisted
on Judith and the wagon. They were a critical part
of the disguise both Doc and Raider knew they'd
need.

Doc was idly turning these reflections over in his
mind when, from somewhere beyond a low rise
just ahead, there was the unmistakable sound of
gunfire.

Raider, on the yellow-tan horse, pulled up short
and stared in that direction.

Doc pulled Judith to a halt. "What the hell's
that?"

"What are you askin' *me* for?" said Raider, still
staring.

Wasting no more words, Doc sprang down from
the wagon seat and rushed to the rear of the vehicle, where his own sorrel gelding was trailing on a
lead rope, already saddled. In a moment he had
mounted and was pummeling along in Raider's
wake toward the crest of the rise.

The chamiso, some of it as much as four feet
high here, helped to camouflage the two riders
as they reached the line of the rise, though it did
not conceal them entirely. Raider pulled up hard
and Doc, overtaking, came alongside him. In the
shallow declivity ahead, no more than two hundred
yards off, several pack and riding animals were
bunched together, a man and woman—as far as
Doc and Raider could make out—standing in the
dust beside them. They were loosely surrounded by

riders, two of whom were dismounting to approach them more closely. Six altogether, it looked like.

"Bandidos," said Raider, peering. "The shots were to scare them two pilgrims, I reckon."

Doc nodded. "I heard in Santa Fe they were thicker than prairie dogs up here."

"Six ain't too thick," Raider said dryly. "But maybe too many just to ride into 'em whoopin' and hollerin'."

Doc glanced at him. "Are you thinking what I'm thinking?"

"Yup. Guess you and me, Doc, are gonna do like the Apaches do."

No more explanation was needed. Both men dismounted, pulled their horses back out of sight, overheading their reins so they'd stay in place as they were trained to do—at least so Doc and Raider had assumed when they'd bought them, fairly well used, from the livery stable in Santa Fe—and then, crouching, they moved forward through the wiry, juniper-like bushes toward the gathering down the slope.

Raider unholstered his Colt .44. Doc had his Diamondback .38, with its shorter, four-and-a-half-inch barrel, in his hand. The Von Lengerke & Antoine catalog, out of Chicago, claimed the Diamondback was ideal for policemen and other officers of the law, though Raider sometimes snorted at it and called it a toy. If it was, Doc always retorted, it played some pretty deadly damned games.

The situation below became clearer as Doc and Raider, making zigzag patterns, keeping low and in partial cover, approached the people and horses below. The first thing Doc noticed was that the female person who was one of the two accosted by the bandits was, well, more than just any old female person. At least, to his eyes, and at this distance, she was. Tall, to begin with—almost Raider's height, and he was six-foot-two. Maybe a hair taller than Doc himself. Her pale, golden hair, close to the color of a buttercup, was done up, out of the way, in some kind of bun in back that would no doubt have a fancy French name, though Doc, for the moment, couldn't recall it. As for that figure of hers, in a loose checked blouse and a long gray skirt with buttons down the front, well, it was every bit as good as those you saw in marble in museums, wearing nothing at all. Maybe a shade slimmer, which, as far as he was concerned, made it even better. Except not slim everywhere. Even that loose shirtwaist of hers didn't conceal those burgeoning breasts, which protruded forward almost like the horns of a wild Mexican bull.

The other pilgrim, except for the trail dust that covered him, looked just as much out of place here among the mesas. He was an older man, slender, slow-moving, an off-white linen wagonduster falling to his knees, a tweed cap with fore-and-aft visors on his head—the kind Englishmen wore to go shooting grouse, Doc reflected—and with what Doc, even at this distance, sensed as a vague and kind of bewildered look in his eyes, as though he dimly realized what was happening to him but wished it would hurry up and be over with so he could get on with more important things.

The squat, toadlike man who was holding his hat out to the two pilgrims, as they dropped things from their pockets into it, acted like the leader of the *bandidos*. Hovering behind him was a razor-thin hombre who was probably his principal lieutenant. The other four bandits, all dismounted, were going through the packs on the packhorses, scattering clothes, blankets, and other articles into the dust. All were too busy to notice that Doc and Raider were now almost upon them.

Long used to working with each other, Doc and Raider traded no remarks as they came side by side behind a small outcropping of rock with fronds of chamiso growing from the cracks in it. There would be a moment, both sensed, when they'd act together, but that moment wasn't quite upon them yet. It would be when all six of the bandits had their attention fully diverted, with none able to make a lightning response as the two Pinkerton men announced their presence. They waited, listening; they were close enough now to hear voices.

The toadlike man said, "Tha's all you got?" His accent was Spanish.

"That's everything!" said the girl, coldly. Her voice was well modulated—a finishing-school accent, Doc thought. "And now will you kindly go away and let us continue our journey?"

The toadlike man glanced at his thin companion and grinned. "You hear that, Transito? She says she don't got no more."

The thin man's voice was dry and had cracks in it. "Oh, I think she got more, Cristóbal. That is what I think."

"That is what I also think," said Cristóbal, holding his grin.

With that, he whirled abruptly back toward the girl, stepped toward her, and, before she could realize what was happening, reached forward and ripped open the front of her shirtwaist. Her breasts, unsupported by any undergarment, came tumbling out. It was Doc's guess that she found corsets and such uncomfortable—or else they just didn't make anything big enough to accommodate them. They were, he told himself with a slight, indrawn breath, a magnificent set of melons. Swelling, creamy white, the huge discs around the nipples a virginal peach color . . .

Doc was impressed with the way the girl stood there, stock still, staring back at the toadlike bandit icily, keeping herself erect and with her shoulders squared. Her companion, the older man, made a slow clumsy turn toward Cristóbal, reaching out as though to try restraining him—he had bottom, though not much muscle to back it up, Doc reflected—and the thin man stepped forward and swung his pistol viciously across the side of the old man's head, knocking him into the dust.

Both Cristóbal and Transito at once turned upon the girl. Laughing, they grabbed her and threw her down upon the ground. Transito, at her head, held her down with his hands on her breasts, his fingers working on her nipples at the same time until they hardened involuntarily and began to stick up out of the discs like hard, pale little cherries. Toadlike Cristóbal dropped his pants, which wouldn't go easily over his boots, so he left them there, crumpled around his ankles, and awkwardly threw himself upon the supine woman, tearing at the line of buttons in front of her skirt, and then shoving up the white, lace-edged petticoat under it. Doc glimpsed the smudge of hair between her legs —as golden as that on her head—and the salmon-pink labial flesh in the crack between it as Cristóbal sought to force her apart with his rough fingers. His cock was already out of the fly of his longjohns, thick and stubby, erect at an angle. He scrambled upward upon her and began trying to thrust it in.

"Hey, hurry up, Cristóbal!" cried the thin bandit, laughing, still holding the girl down. "I want my turn!"

Although all of this was enough to draw Doc's full attention, he was also—in some astonishment

—watching the girl herself. She had not said a word since both men had leapt upon her. She had not fought them back. She had made herself cold and rigid; almost unbelievably, she kept her eyes open and stared upon her attackers with venomous hate. In her acceptance of the fact that neither protest nor struggle would have done her any good at all she was displaying a hard logic Doc had not seen many women employ—nor many men, come to think of it. He didn't know which to admire more: her coolness in this situation or the magnificent perfection of those great breasts of hers.

The other four bandits had stopped looting the packhorses and were gathered around the girl and the two men atop her, watching, grinning, no doubt awaiting their turn.

The moment had come.

Doc and Raider glanced quickly at each other, Raider nodded, and then both rose and stepped forward, their weapons in their hands and pointed.

"I reckon that'll be enough, *compadres*," said Raider. His voice was almost conversational, but the hardness of steel lay just below it.

One bandit, off to the left, tried to swing his rifle, which looked like an old Henry single-shot carbine, toward Raider and Doc. The muzzle of Raider's .44 shifted slightly as he pointed, rather than aimed—which any gunfighter worth his salt has to learn to do—and then the gun spoke, startlingly loud in the hot silence, bucking upward slightly in recoil in Raider's hand.

The bandit's rifle, struck on the end of its stock, was knocked out of his hand.

"Drop all of 'em," said Raider. "Pronto."

Weapons clattered to the ground. Doc went forward and collected them as Raider stood there, his hogleg still pointed.

"And you," Raider said to Cristóbal, who was still supporting himself on his hands and knees over the girl, his stubby cock hanging limply now, "get up, you sonofabitch. Get up and button your drawers."

"Si, si," said the stocky bandit, moving hastily. "Hey, señor, we do not mean anything bad. Just a little joke, no? *Un chiste—"*

"Shut up," said Raider wearily, and the man did.

There was a passage of moments in which the bandits were herded together and off to one side by gun gestures. Some looked surprised, some looked annoyed, some looked resentful. Cristóbal, especially, glared at Raider angrily. Doc assisted as, at Raider's command, they all returned what they'd stolen, including a gold railroad watch on a chain that had evidently belonged to the older man. He had risen shakily to his feet by now, daubing the slight gash on the side of his forehead with the tips of his fingers and still looking, in some strange way, as though he were observing all this rather than actually taking part in it.

"Get on your nags, señores," Raider said sardonically. "Show your faces again and I'll blast 'em all to hell without even thinkin' about it. Savvy? Okay. That's it. Vamoose!"

The bandits mounted. Hooves clattered. Doc and Raider watched them disappear over the rise through the settling dust.

The girl was on her feet again. She had gathered together the buttonfronts of both her shirt and skirt as best she could. The edges of her breasts were still visible, and, Doc thought a little dryly, a pleasant sight he was just as happy to behold.

"I'm Genevieve Ashley, gentlemen," she said, facing them. "I just don't know how to thank you."

"I could think of some ways," said Doc, the remark coming out before he could rein it in. Raider glanced at him quickly, which was maybe meant to warn him to hold his tongue—at least for the time being.

Raider nodded to acknowledge the girl's self-introduction. "I'm Raider. This is Doc Weatherbee. Now, lady, tell me something. Just what in the hell are a couple of greenhorns like you two doing riding alone in country like this?"

The girl sighed. "I'm afraid that's a long story."

"About lunchtime," said Raider, glancing up at the sun. "Suppose we all set a spell and hear it."

CHAPTER TWO

Raider made cowboy coffee, throwing the ground beans into the pot just as the water came to a boil. The tiny fire of gathered pinyon sticks below it burned flamelessly in the bright sun, giving off very little smoke. By now Doc and Raider had brought their wagon to the site where the bandits had stopped the two pilgrims. And by now Genevieve Ashley—a little to Doc's disappointment—had had a chance to duck behind some rocks and arrange herself a little more modestly.

The older man was Jonathan Ashley, Genevieve's father. He still looked vaguely absent-minded about all that had just taken place. He had retrieved his double-billed grouse-shooting hat and returned it to his head, which was covered with long, wavy, but largely uncombed white hair. He had been allowing Genevieve to do most of the talking, nodding now and then to affirm what she said.

Raider leaned back, sipping the hot coffee from his tin cup. He had a thin, twisted cheroot going, and was listening attentively to Genevieve Ashley's explanation, which was coming in bits and pieces.

"So, you see," said Genevieve, picking up where she'd left off after the last interruption, "not being able to obtain funds from the university itself—or from any other source—Father decided to carry out the expedition on his own."

"Let me get this straight now," said Raider. "It's some kind of Spanish treasure you're after?"

For the first time Jonathan Ashley raised his

head and showed some signs of animation. It was obvious that the conversation had come around to his favorite subject. "Not treasure in the ordinary sense, young man," he said to Raider, addressing him as though he were a student—which was maybe the way he addressed everyone—"but as far as scholarly worth is concerned, a treasure far beyond any monetary value."

"There are such things, I suppose," said Doc. His little sigh also said that he didn't imagine there were many, though.

"As Genevieve told you," Ashley continued, "my field is history. I teach a little, of course, but most of my time is spent in research. Which, more and more, necessitates considerable travel. A certain alumnus of my own university—Harvard—has shown that there is no substitute for visiting the location of a primary source—that is to say, documents or records directly concerned with the incident or period one wishes to recreate. This is William Prescott, who died shortly before the late struggle between the States, and, by spending years abroad, produced that magnificent volume *The Conquest of Peru.*"

Doc looked puzzled. "What kind of documents would you be hoping to find out here, way past West Hell and gone?"

"Not documents, precisely," said Professor Ashley. "I've already uncovered most of the records pertaining to this matter. Some in Madrid, some in Mexico City, and even certain corollary records in Santa Fe. It's the artifacts themselves I'm after now. Although the research grants committee was too shortsighted to finance the expedition, I've at least been given sabbatical leave so that I can look for this deposit on my own. When it's found—if it is—we'll know a great deal more about the history of this territory and, indeed, of all the Southwest."

"I didn't think there was much in the way of history here," said Doc. "Never been enough people around to make much history. Kit Carson and the mountain men coming to Taos for rendezvous in the thirties, maybe, and Colonel Doniphan, out of Missouri, leading his volunteers down into Mexico in '47—"

"Father's period is much earlier than that," said Genevieve. "The conquistadores. Coronado, and his expedition up the Rio Grande in 1540—well over three hundred years ago. Many of the people in this area are descendants of the Spaniards who came this far north at that time."

"So they left some stuff you hope to find in Tesqua, is that it?" asked Raider.

"Not Tesqua," said Ashley, shaking his head. "One of the nearby Indian pueblos. Armor. Weapons, perhaps. Everyday articles such as cooking pots or religious talismans. From these we can tell a great deal about the people who used them."

Genevieve interrupted her father. "That's really all we should tell about it, Father," she said. "We do want to get to the site before anybody else does, after all."

Raider smiled. "You can trust us, Miss Ashley. Doc and I ain't studyin' on beating you to some collection of old cooking pots."

"Of course, gentlemen," she said quickly. "I didn't mean to impugn your integrity in the slightest. But the more information we give out, the greater the chance that it will spread and that someone else will go looking for our archaeological treasure. And for someone else to find it would be disastrous for Father. They were reluctant to grant him leave for this purpose, you see—there were some who quarreled with his findings. There's more jealousy and backbiting in the academic world than you could possibly imagine. If Father fails in this he may even lose his tenure. If he succeeds, of course, he'll enjoy advancement in his career." What seemed a wry smile flickered across her face momentarily. "Father trusts others too much; I have to watch out for him."

"Genevieve exaggerates," said Ashley. He glanced at her fondly. "Still, I'm delighted to have her along. She takes care of things I'm rather bad at. Remembering train tickets, keeping appointments, having my notes in order—"

"In short," said Genevieve, laughing a little, "Father would forget his head if it weren't attached to him."

"As I say," said Ashley, smiling, "she exaggerates."

"Well," said Raider, pinching off the light at the end of his cheroot and tucking the remainder into his pocket for later smoking, "there's one thing maybe you both forgot. And that's the fact that tenderfeet just shouldn't travel in these parts without some kind of protection. It starts to get kinda lawless this far up the Brazos. As I reckon you just found out. I think Doc and I better tag along with you the rest of the way. If that's agreeable."

"More than agreeable, Mr. Raider," said Genevieve. "Indeed, we are most grateful."

It was now a small caravan winding northward, at times crossing the sparsely vegetated, harshly eroded land where the wagon trail led, now and then skirting the deeply cut river itself, on occasion passing through tiny settlements of adobe *jacales* where the descendants of Coronado's sol-

diers—as Doc and Raider realized more fully now
—kept their sheep and goats and vegetable patches.

Genevieve sat beside Doc on the wagon. Raider
and Professor Ashley, mounted, trailed behind with
the packhorses.

She settled back on the seat almost languidly.
Doc was acutely aware of the warmth of her magnificent body beside him—brushing against him
once in a while, and giving him the same trouble
Raider had complained of earlier, making him
wonder if, by casually glancing at his lap, she
might not notice.

"This *is* more comfortable than riding, I must
admit," said Genevieve.

" 'Specially riding sidesaddle," said Doc, glancing at her.

"You noticed, then," said Genevieve.

"Couldn't help but," said Doc. "Not very practical out here, where you stay in the saddle all day.
If I were you, Miss Genevieve, I'd get me a pair of
pants and ride like anybody else."

"You're right, of course," she said earnestly. "It's
just that back east the sidesaddle's more ladylike,
I suppose. I didn't really think about it. Some of
Father's absentmindedness must be rubbing off
on me."

"You seem to be pretty close to him," said Doc.

She nodded—and there was the sense of a sigh
in it. "Since Mother died. I don't know what he'd
do without me."

"But I expect you're going to have to leave him
sometime."

"I suppose so." A tiny frown appeared between
her eyes as she stared ahead at the trail. "I might
as well tell you, Dr. Weatherbee, that the subject's
come up from time to time."

"Make it Doc," said Doc. "I'm a self-trained

veterinarian, but not really a doctor. Anyway, how did the subject come up?"

"Well, there have been swains. Times when I thought I might get married, settle down, have my own home. The sort of thing I suppose every woman wants, in her heart. But I could never bring myself to leave Father. He needs me too much. Or maybe I wasn't really in love with any of the young men who came along." She glanced at Doc. "None of them was as—what shall I say?—as assured or capable as you and your partner seem to be."

Doc smiled a little. "You get assured and capable pretty quick out here. You won't last long if you don't."

"In fact," said Genevieve, still looking at him closely, "I have the feeling that both of you are capable of more than driving a medicine wagon from town to town. I gather that's what you do, isn't it? Sell your medicine—put on some kind of show, I suppose?"

Doc shrugged. "A man's got to do something to make a living. Since we both like to keep moving, this seemed to be a good way." He tried not to let her see his own little frown. The girl was sharper than he'd given her credit for, and it just wouldn't do for her to see through his and Raider's elaborate disguise.

Later in the afternoon, Professor Ashley joined Genevieve on the wagon to give his own buttocks, unaccustomed to the saddle, a respite, and Doc and Raider rode together, side by side.

"Not bad, that Genevieve," said Doc, somewhat laconically.

Raider nodded and smiled a little. "I'd make a play for her myself if she looked at me the way she looks at you."

"Hadn't noticed," said Doc.

"Bullshit," said Raider. "Your eyes get a hard-on every time you turn 'em her way. Well, partner, she's all yours. And I wouldn't back off that easy for just anybody."

"Trouble is," said Doc, "I'm not a hundred percent sure about her."

"About gettin' into her?"

"Not that. Where she stands, I mean. Both her and the professor. That whole queer story of theirs could be an act, just like ours. She seemed a little suspicious of us as a couple of medicine men."

Raider nodded. "We might as well be careful. About anybody. Though I don't see how they figure into what we're doing. It's possible, I guess, but it don't seem likely this Magrue hombre got wind of us."

"I don't imagine he would through any of the Pinks—Willy in Denver, or Allan himself, in Chicago, probably wouldn't advise anyone else in the organization what's up. But, remember, it's the Department of the Interior who contracted out to us on this matter, and there's no telling what those dunderheads in Washington might do. Either shooting off their mouths too much or actually being in cahoots with somebody like Seth Magrue."

"Could be," said Raider. "Only it'd be hard for anybody to get word to Magrue up in Tesqua—at least not real fast. No telegraph, no stage service, mail rider maybe once a week. That's how he gets away with what he's allegedly doin'. Off to one side and half forgot. It'd look too suspicious to him if they sent their own investigators in, and that's why they turned to the agency."

"Well," said Doc, "let's just sit tight and see what happens."

"Yup," said Raider. " 'Bout like we always do."

They rode silently for a while, and Doc thought

about the Pinkerton National Detective Agency, for which they both worked. Born in Scotland, Allan Pinkerton had come to America in the forties, made his reputation running down a gang of counterfeiters in Illinois, uncovered a plot to assassinate President Lincoln in Baltimore in 1861, and then had been appointed as Lincoln's military intelligence chief during the war. He hadn't been too successful at this, constantly exaggerating the strength of Lee's army, but, returning to crime detection after the war, he had accomplished a number of coups, such as finding the thieves who took $700,000 from the Adams Express Company in 1866, and managed to expand his now nationwide and highly reputed organization. Both Raider and Doc had met him in Chicago, finding him old and a bit crotchety, and suspecting he didn't have much time left, but knowing the organization he'd built would keep going for some years to come. Which suited both men to a *T*. What Doc had told Genevieve about the way they liked to keep moving was the absolute truth, even if the part about the medicine wagon wasn't.

The sun reddened the sky as it sank in the west. Streaks of distant, dying purple clouds hung over the spine of the Great Divide, crossing its pasted-wafer disc. They chose a sandy spot along the river near a grove of tamaracks for their overnight camp. Raider and Doc gathered the wood, with the professor trying to help but mostly getting in the way, and Genevieve did the cooking—with somewhat more care than either Raider or Doc would have given the chore, Doc had to admit. From the salt pork and dried beans they carried, and from some fresh, bright red chile powder she'd stopped to buy in one of the little settlements, along with a clove of garlic, she made a delicious concoction that warmed the innards as it went down. Doc and Raider ate this appreciatively and with appropriate nods and murmurs; the professor put his own meal down mechanically, obviously scarcely tasting it, his mind no doubt on the archaeological treasure he was supposed to be seeking.

"I'll take the first watch, Rade," Doc said after it had become dark.

"If you like," Raider shrugged. "I'll turn in now. You can wake me 'long about midnight."

"Shouldn't I take watch, too?" asked the professor, lifting his head.

"Better if Doc and I do it," said Raider, smiling slightly. "We got more experience. No offense, Professor."

"Well . . . if you insist," said Ashley. He yawned.

In a trice, Raider was stretched out under a blanket, his head on his saddle, his eyes closed, a gentle snore beginning. Doc marveled anew at his ability to sleep at will, even in the saddle, or on a bed of spikes, for all Doc knew. The professor found his own blankets in his packs, and, luxury of luxuries, a genuine pillow, and before long he was in slumberland, too, obviously quite tired after his somewhat eventful day.

Doc, a rifle in his crossed arms, found a place in a cluster of rocks a little upslope from the river, where he had a good view of most of the surrounding terrain, squatted there, and lit himself a clay pipe. About once a day was plenty for the pipe; he'd be unable to replenish his small store of Richmond Sweet Burley, once it ran out, in these parts.

The moon rose, three-quarters full, bright, and faintly adipose, like candle wax. Stars were crushed diamonds in the immense, blue-black sky.

Up the slope, moving gracefully like a floating wraith in the moonlight, came Genevieve Ashley.

Doc had kind of figured she would.

"Peaceful out here," she said, lowering herself to a sitting position beside Doc. "And such a big sky . . . such a lovely sky."

He nodded. "I knew it was for me, first time I saw it. I'm from New York City, you know, just like Billy the Kid. New York's all right, I guess, but as Rade says, it just don't have room to cuss a cat in."

She laughed dutifully. "I can understand why you don't want to be tied down—confined. It's a little different with a woman, though. Most of us want a home in one place. A sanctuary, I suppose, that's always there."

"I daresay that has its advantages," said Doc. He was studying her. Well, not exactly studying. Just enjoying what he'd already studied pretty thoroughly all day. That Viking-goddess profile of hers —like the ones you saw, white alabaster against pink coral, on cameo brooches. Those strong, curved shoulders, a little broader than those of most women. And those incredible breasts, straining now against even the loose containment of the off-shoulder Mexican blouse she'd changed into— one she'd picked up in Santa Fe, he'd guess. "For example," he continued, "what a man wants would be always there, waiting for him."

"Yes." Her eyes were very intent upon him now. "What a man wants. And, though not many of them admit it, what a woman wants, too."

Doc needed no more encouragement than that. He reached forward, slowly, gently, drawing it out to prolong the pleasure, put his hand on her half-bared shoulder, and slid the filmy blouse away from it. Quickly and gracefully she wriggled her arm out of the sleeve so that the blouse came off all the way. One breast was now fully exposed. It swelled outward, cream-white in the moonlight, soft and yet taut, as though it were a toy balloon blown almost to the bursting point. The nipple stood up, pointed and saucy, like a walnut-sized nubbin of gutta-percha, in its broad pink nest, at least twice the diameter of a silver dollar.

Doc brought his head down and forward and put his mouth to the nubbin of her breast. He sucked a little and rolled his tongue upon it until she gasped with pleasure, then took him by the back of the head and pressed him harder into herself. His free hand went down to just above her knees and began to crumple her skirt up and out of the way, his palm at the same time enjoying the silken smoothness of her thigh. In a moment his fingers had found her soft, moist quim, and with his middle finger he began to lightly stroke the tiny button of the clitoris he found at the top of the warm, dark valley between her legs.

"Doc!" she half groaned, half whispered, her eyes rolling.

"Yes, Jenny?"

"Fuck me slowly. Ever so slowly. Not all at once, but slowly—"

"I was figuring on just that," Doc said dryly. He brought his head up from her breast, then put his lips on hers as she parted them slightly to receive his darting, exploring tongue, entwining it with her own in a serpentine mating dance. He broke away from the kiss presently and helped her as she hastily removed the rest of her clothes, stripping himself of what he wore with intermittent motions.

Her fabulous body was stretched out before him. Her hands were behind her head, which exposed her soft armpits and pulled up her great globes of breasts so that the nipples pointed upward, toward the diamond-studded sky. Her eyes half-closed now, she murmured, "Shakespeare—"

"Shakespeare?" said Doc, puzzled. "What the hell?"

"From *Venus and Adonis*. 'Graze on my lips; and if those hills be dry . . . Stray lower, where the pleasant fountains lie.' "

"Oh," said Doc. "Guess old Willy knew more about it than I gave him credit for."

She laughed softly.

Following the bard's dictum, Doc strayed lower. His lips brushed downward along her smooth, rolling abdomen, pausing a moment at her navel to dart his tongue into it playfully. In a moment he was kissing and breathing hot upon her nest of darker golden hair. His flickering tongue found the man in the boat, stroked it. She writhed convulsively, coming, gasping with it.

Doc's erection was straining at its prepuce, turning it purple, as though about to burst it in one great explosion. She reached down and grabbed it. Hard. It took all the skill he possessed to keep from coming, then and there. With her other hand, she pulled his head away and writhed about, reversing herself; then she closed down upon his eight-inch penis—now as hard and thick as a braided whip handle—with her full mouth, taking it as far back as she could, rolling her tongue on the sensitive little string at the base of its head, bringing him to the edge of blackout as the maddening thrill surged up from his groin and turned every drop of his blood to bubbly water, like in a lemon phosphate.

She sensed it whenever he was about to come and desisted for a moment, giving him a chance to recover. Doc wasn't sure how long this went on— it felt like most of forever. Not only his prick, but his entire well-muscled body was now at the bursting point.

"All right, Doc, darling," she whispered at last, between gasps, "time to put it in."

"Thought we'd never get to it," said Doc. He rolled himself around to get on top of her.

"No—wait," she said. She turned and rested herself on her hands and knees, exposing her magnificently curved backside. "Doggy fashion," she said. "It's wonderful that way when the man's long enough to reach it. And you, Doc, are. And then some, I'm happy to say."

Crouching on his knees, Doc eased his member in; his own sensitive part rubbed past her clitoris as it went in. Her gasp, when that happened, almost reached the level of a scream of joy. He reached forward and cupped her hanging breasts in his hands, rolling the nipples in his fingers. Then he shoved as hard as he could and went all the way in. She wriggled and writhed, her vulva closing down upon him as though to suck him dry, and he pumped hard, back and forth, keeping the strokes short enough to prevent him from slipping out again.

"Now!" she cried suddenly. "Oh, Doc, my darling —*now!*"

He gave one final shove and held it there. The life poured out of him, wet and thick, and into her, mingling with her own juices, and she cried aloud in all-but-swooning pleasure as it did so.

CHAPTER THREE

Doc was a little disappointed to learn that Genevieve and her father, having inquired in Santa Fe
about accommodations in the little town of Tesqua, had received the name of a *casa de huéspedes*
—a kind of boardinghouse—and had decided to
stay there instead of at La Posada, the settlement's
only inn. After he and Raider had deposited the
Ashleys safely in their new quarters, they turned
back toward the center of town to put up their
horses in the livery stable and take a hotel room
for themselves.

The inn was on the town's central plaza, which
was built around a square, parklike patch planted
with cactus instead of grass because of the dry
climate, and the town's major buildings were on
its perimeter, facing inward. The sidewalks in front
of the buildings were given shade by protruding
roofs supported by *vigas,* or long poles acting as
beams, and many of these were festooned with
strings of bright red chile peppers or dried, painted
gourds. They locked the wagon and left it parked
near the stable, then proceeded on foot to the plaza
and the inn.

Some kind of festival seemed to be going on in
the plaza. There were musicians in the center with
guitars and fiddles, and two dancers, dressed in
Spanish costumes, were performing on a platform
in front of them, tapping their heels and clicking
castanets. A fair-to-middling crowd had gathered
in the square. Most, by their dress—loose, light
garments of coarse weave—seemed to be of Span-

28

ish descent, though there were a number of men and women in more ordinary American rural garb. Scattered through the crowd were also a number of Indians with blankets wrapped around their jeans, covering their buttocks. Doc had heard that for convenience they cut holes in the backs of their store-bought pants to make them more like their former traditional trousers and then used the blankets to cover the apertures.

The inn—a low adobe structure like nearly all those in Tesqua—was across the plaza, and Doc and Raider headed toward it.

"It's that bath I'm lookin' forward to," said Raider. "They better have one."

"I expect they will," said Doc. "Most of 'em look washed around here. More than in some cow and mining towns I've seen."

"And then a woman to curl up with a spell."

"Judging from all the kids running around," Doc said dryly, "they've got them, too."

They passed a browned, grizzled, stocky man who, hat in hand, was quietly watching the dancers. Raider paused. "Hey, señor," he said, "what's goin' on here today, anyway?"

"*No hablo inglés*," said the man, blinking rheumy eyes.

A taller man with short-cropped white hair, wearing a Spanish suit embroidered with gold braid, turned toward Doc and Raider, evidently overhearing the exchange. His sweeping white mustaches curved outward like the boss of a longhorn. "You will forgive me, señores," he said courteously. "I can answer your question. It is the festival of San Ysidro, the town's patron saint."

"Thank you kindly," said Raider. "Figured it was something like that."

"You are, of course, strangers to Tesqua." The

white-haired man was examining them more closely. His features were delicate, aristocratic—almost
transparent, like fine porcelain, thought Doc.

"That we are," said Raider, nodding, returning
the man's close examination, obviously in order to
decide whether to volunteer any information beyond that.

"Then allow me to welcome you." The man
bowed slightly. "I am Don Luis Mondragon."

"Howdy. I'm Raider; this is Doc Weatherbee."

"Is there some person in particular you seek
here? Perhaps I can help you find him." The words
were casual, but the old man's searching eyes were
not. Clearly, he had more than a passing interest in
whatever reasons would bring strangers to Tesqua.

"Nobody in particular," said Raider. "You might
say we're just driftin' through."

"I see," said Don Luis. He showed a faint smile.
"Of course, after passing through Tesqua, there
are not many places to drift to, are there?"

"So I've heard," said Raider. "Well, thanks for
the information. We'll see you around, I reckon."

"Hasta entonces, señores," said Don Luis, bowing again.

Although its architecture was Spanish, the inn
basically offered the facilities of any hotel, anywhere, with—as Doc and Raider presently discovered—one exception. They were led to a pleasant room with an outside door that opened upon a
courtyard. A galvanized tub was carried in and
servants, making several trips, filled it with hot water. A plump and pretty maid fetched the bottle of
Millikan's Squirrel Whiskey they ordered. Within
an hour or so both men were bathed and refreshed
and had changed into clean clothes. Because of the
warmth, Doc wore only a pearl-gray vest and no
jacket over it; Raider donned a loose, flowing, oys-

ter-white shirt with a thonged placket at its neck. They made their way to the cantina, which was in a darker, cooler room in one wing of the posada. They could have continued to sip the Millikan's in the privacy of their room, of course, but in Tesqua, as in any town, there would be more information available in the bar, so their sojourn there was in the nature of a reconnaissance.

The bartender had a moon face and wore owlish, steel-rimmed glasses, fastened to his ears with little black strings. There were perhaps a dozen drinkers scattered throughout the tables in the room, some glancing at Doc and Raider as they entered, but most, on the whole, minding their own business.

Raider spotted the kegs behind the bar, with their coils going through water-soaked burlap, and ordered beer. Doc did the same.

"Si, señores," said the bartender. *"Dos cervezas."*

The beer was moderately cool rather than ice cold, but it did slake their thirst, which the dust of the trail had exacerbated somewhat.

"Kinda quiet in here," Raider said to the bartender.

"Si." The bartender nodded. "Everyone, he is out watching the festival."

"Even the girls?"

"What girls, señor?"

"I think you know what I mean," said Raider, with the suggestion of a smile.

"Ah! *That* kind!" said the bartender. He busied himself polishing a glass. (Was there a bartender anywhere, wondered Doc, who didn't polish glasses while he was talking to you?) "Well, señor, we do not have that kind here in the cantina. You will have to find the guesthouse of Señora Valdez at the far end of town. It is the only place. Señor Magrue

does not permit the keeping of such girls elsewhere."

"And who might Señor Magrue be?" Raider
glanced at Doc to keep him from blurting out that
he knew damned well who Señor Magrue was—
his question was merely for the purpose of probing.

The bartender shrugged. "The *patrón* of all the
town. You will do well to remember it while you're
here."

"You mean he's the mayor or something like
that?"

"No, no, señor. He is the Indian agent for all the
pueblos out there." He waved vaguely to indicate
the surrounding countryside. "But that is only his
trabajo—his job, no? There is a mayor, Señor
Higgins, and a sheriff, Señor Busby, and other officials, all of them Anglo, but it is Señor Magrue who
controls them. And everybody else."

"I take it you don't cotton much to this setup,"
said Raider, studying the bartender.

The man shrugged deeply and expressively
again. "One works. One tries to make a living. One
is careful not to stir up a nest of bees."

"Is that," asked Doc, "how most of the Mexicans
around here feel about it?"

The bartender drew himself up, and answered
pleasantly enough, though it was obviously an
effort on his part not to show that his fur had been
rubbed the wrong way a little. "We are not Mexicans, señor. We are Spanish. Descendants of the
conquistadores."

Doc nodded. "All right. Spanish. I'll remember
that. No offense."

"None was taken, señor. *Un otra vez*? Two more
beers?"

"Might as well," said Raider.

They sipped their second round of beers as the

bartender busied himself with other customers. "Well," said Doc, alone with Raider again, "how do you figure we ought to tackle this?"

"First thing we've got to do is act natural," Raider said. "Just like we're really here to peddle that medicine. Get a good night's sleep, set up the wagon in the morning. I've an idea this Magrue hombre'll come pokin' around soon enough—we won't have to go lookin' for him. When he does we'll do like the Quakers say—'proceed as way opens.'"

Doc nodded. "We ought to be ready to throw a few hints at Magrue that maybe we're not exactly solid citizens. He'll kind of assume that when he sees the medicine wagon, anyway. It might open him up a bit."

"Question is, will it open him enough? He's naturally keepin' his shady activities close to the vest—even if everybody in town has a pretty good idea what's goin' on. What I mean is, he's not leavin' anything hangin' out that could be used as proof. And that's what we're after. Proof."

"True enough," said Doc. "Maybe that's one thing you can say good about the government. They lean over backward to be fair. Just rumors that he's selling off the stuff they send out for the Indians aren't enough. We've got to catch him more or less red-handed."

"Surprises me he hasn't been caught at it already," said Raider reflectively. "It can't be easy to take food stores and dry goods and hardware and agricultural implements, like big plows and everything, and just make 'em disappear. To say nothing of the paperwork—receipts and such—he has to come up with. I wonder that the Indians themselves haven't complained, gettin' shoddy substitutes or none at all, the way they are."

Doc shrugged. "Probably he's got 'em buffaloed

some way. Either that, or just plumb scared of him. And he *is* way the hell out here where nobody can really keep an eye on him. We'd better walk easy, and not forget we're on *his* home stampin' grounds." Doc drained his beer. "Speakin' of same, are you going to visit this Madame Valdez?"

"I was thinkin' about it," said Raider, frowning. "Powerful urge in my pecker, after all that ridin'. On the other hand—"

"On the other hand, what?"

"Well, it's hard to explain. Any old port in a storm, I reckon, but it just ain't the same when you pay for it. I mean, you always pay for it, one way or the other, but the cold business of layin' down the cash, hoppin' on, then hoppin' off again—well, you know what I mean."

"I know what you mean," said Doc, smiling. "Not much better'n flogging it. Maybe you should just look around some more and see what you can do elsewhere."

"Easy enough for you to say. You've got Genevieve."

"Maybe. Though maybe not exactly like I want."

"What the hell's that supposed to mean?"

"She shows signs of being serious. A man could get himself tied down that way."

"I sure sympathize with your troubles, Doc," said Raider, grinning sarcastically. "Well, let's have another beer and go out and watch the fiesta."

Although both Raider and Doc were taking pains to seem outwardly calm, each man was inwardly chafing at the bit—anxious to get started on the assignment Willy Pinkerton had given them in Denver. But to stroll around the town, watching the activities of the fiesta, was actually a start, as unproductive as it seemed, for, by doing this, they

were establishing themselves in their roles as new-
ly arrived medicine drummers who would presently begin to peddle their wares.

The fiesta seemed to revolve around the carrying
of a plaster-cast statue of St. Ysidro from place to
place in the town. In each place it would be set
down momentarily for a round of singing and dancing, the waving of colored ribbons, and the throwing of painted eggs, which had been sucked dry
and filled with perfumed water. Doc and Raider
were struck by several of these cheerful missiles,
some thrown by laughing señoritas, and it might
have led to introductions—the first step in what
Raider felt he needed—but all the young ladies
seemed either well accompanied by family mem-
bers or else were much too young and innocent.

The afternoon shadows were long again when
both men returned to the plaza to ready themselves
for dinner at the inn. More musicians and dancers
had gathered there for the evening revelries. As
they crossed the square they saw Genevieve Ashley emerge from a low building kitty-corner to the
inn, a burly, bald-headed man by her side. Sweeping his rakish Stetson from his head and bowing
like a stage actor, he appeared to be seeing her off.
Raider and Doc couldn't pick up too much detail at
this distance, but they had the impression that this
man, with his beaded buckskin jacket and heavy
silver concha belt, was dressed like somebody in a
wild West show. Genevieve nodded in response to
his bow, shook his hand, then turned and came
down the walk under the *portales* while the man
himself stared after her for a moment and presently reentered the door from which he'd emerged.

Doc and Raider changed course so they'd intercept Genevieve. She'd evidently taken Doc's advice
and changed to pants now, but she looked just as

good in them as she had in her buttoned skirt—
maybe even better.

"Well! Gentlemen! Hello again!" said Genevieve.

"Howdy," said Raider. "Looks like you got all
squared away."

Doc and Genevieve glanced at each other and
locked eyes for a moment. It was clear enough to
Raider that they were remembering the pleasures
they'd given each other, with each, perhaps, wondering how they might bring about a return en-
gagement.

"Who was the dude you just said good-bye to?"
asked Raider.

"Dude? Oh, you must mean Mr. Magrue."

"So *that's* who it was!"

Genevieve's eyebrows rose a little as she sensed
Raider's more-than-passing interest. "Is something
wrong?"

"No, no," Raider said quickly. "Just that we'd
heard he was a pretty important man in town and
we kinda wondered about him. Mind if we walk
you home, Jenny?"

"It would be a pleasure," Genevieve said.

They strolled, three abreast, Genevieve in the
middle, toward the dusty main street that led to
the guesthouse where she was staying. Doc, acci-
dentally brushing against Jenny now and then, felt
his blood simmer. He had an idea Raider was having the same reaction—and couldn't really blame
him.

"I suppose, as you say," said Genevieve, "that
Mr. Magrue is one of Tesqua's more distinguished
citizens, but I must confess I did not find him particularly helpful."

"Helpful in what?" asked Doc.

"Well, I went to him to see whether he had any
information about the several pueblos in this area.

Something that might help Father decide which one contains the artifacts he's looking for. You see, as we understand it, one of the tribes considered the Spanish soldiers that visited them minor gods —emissaries from the spirit world, so to speak. They took these various effects they left behind and enshrined them in their kiva—much as we might set up a museum, I suppose. The only difficulty is that Father has been unable to determine which pueblo, though he's quite certain it's one of three in the neighborhood."

"You kind of explained this before," said Raider. "So what about Magrue? He didn't know anything, I take it?"

"Not only that," said Genevieve, "but he tried to discourage us from looking. Mere rumor and superstition, he said. He's been to all the pueblos, of course, as Indian agent, and he said there's nothing in any of them even remotely resembling what we're after. He was polite, of course—even genial —but I had the feeling he strongly wished to discourage us."

"As though he didn't want you poking around?" Raider glanced at her.

She nodded. "Yes. That was the impression I got. Rather disappointing. Father had hoped he'd cooperate—perhaps even take us to the pueblos and intercede for us there. Instead he said the best thing we could do would be to turn around and go back home."

"Which I don't reckon you're going to do."

"Not on your tintype," said Genevieve, nodding firmly. "And it's more than just pride. If Father gets back empty-handed his entire career is ruined. He'll be a laughingstock. The worst part of it is he probably won't be able to find another position. I love Father dearly, as you know, but except for teaching and carrying out historical researches, he simply can't *do* anything. And, oh, by the way, Mr. Magrue said you two gentlemen had better be sure to get a permit."

"For what?" asked Doc.

"For selling that medicine of yours."

"You mentioned us to him?"

"Well, of course. I told him how you drove off those bandits. I thought he'd be favorably impressed, and that that might be helpful to you."

"And he wasn't favorably impressed?"

Genevieve frowned slightly. "It's hard to say. He didn't seem to react one way or the other. I had the feeling the news disturbed him—though I can't imagine why."

"Well," said Raider, "what are you and the professor goin' to do now?"

"Continue as we are," said Genevieve. "Father went to the courthouse to examine some records while I went to see Mr. Magrue. We'll try to put everything together this evening and decide on our next move."

Doc glanced at her again. "Does that mean you're kinda tied up tonight?"

She showed him a flickering smile. "I'm afraid so. But, er, I won't be tied up *every* night."

"I reckon I can wait," Doc said, with half a sigh.

It was well after midnight when Doc, who had been dreaming of Genevieve, was awakened by Raider's stirring in the bed beside him, and then by the light of the kerosene lamp that Raider turned on. He blinked sleepily and saw Raider struggling into his pants.

"All right, Rade. Where the hell do you think *you're* going?"

It was hard to tell sometimes when Raider was

grinning, but Doc, looking at him now, thought he might be. They had passed a rather dull evening, dining on spicy enchiladas and bland, mealy *refritos* at the inn, watching the music and dancing in the plaza, and withdrawing finally to the cantina for several rounds of Millikan's Squirrel as a nightcap. Raider had made half a play for the plump, pretty waitress there, but she'd politely explained that she was meeting her *novio* as soon as she finished working—a young aristocrat she hoped to marry as soon as they could persuade his family to approve of her. After that they had yawned several times and decided, what the hell, they both needed a good night's sleep in a real bed.

"Can't hold it in no longer," grunted Raider. "Goin' to see Madame Valdez. You want to come along?"

"I'll check this time," said Doc. "Feels too good right where I am."

"Suit yourself." Raider shrugged and finished dressing.

He stalked through the lobby, nodding at the sleepy night clerk behind the desk, then emerged onto the plaza, which was quiet now and littered with the bunting and broken, colored eggshells left over from the fiesta. The night sky was clear, as usual, glowing with the light of the myriad stars and the high, solemn moon. He found a twisted cheroot in his pocket, thumbnailed a match, lit it, and puffed the fragrant tobacco as he strolled on.

Several minutes later, as he approached the livery stable, horses quiescent in the corral beside it, he saw the medicine wagon where he and Doc had parked it, its whiffletrees resting on two empty barrels to keep it level. The gaudy lettering on its side, decorated by numerous curlicues, was visible in the moonlight. So was the back door of the wagon, which was open—and so was the soft, moving glow of light coming from its interior.

Raider glanced at the surrounding shapes and shadows—the wall of the livery stable, the flank of the building next to it, which contained a grain-and-feed store—saw no other movement, then tiptoed toward the wagon. Unthinkingly, he reached toward his right hip, and when his hand didn't find his holster there he remembered that he'd left the .44 in the hotel room; after all, he hadn't expected to use it at Madame Valdez's. Cursing to himself, he walked even a little softer.

Moments later he had reached the open back doors of the wagon. He was easing his head and shoulders forward to peer inside when he heard a slight puffing sound and the light went out: Whoever was in there had blown out the flame from a carried lantern. Raider drew back a little, but it wasn't quite enough.

A squat, toadlike figure stepped from the wagon, and Raider recognized it immediately as belonging to Cristóbal, the leader of the bandits who had accosted Professor Ashley and Genevieve out on the trail.

Cristóbal saw Raider at about the same time Raider saw him. He dropped his doused kerosene lantern and a sample bottle of De Vere's Tonic, Purifies and Stimulates the Blood—there wasn't much else beyond such samples in the wagon. He reached toward his own hip. Unlike Raider, Cristóbal did have a gun.

CHAPTER FOUR

In a way, you could say that Raider was not a thinking man. Oh, he thought about things, of course—turned them over in his mind from time to time, especially when he didn't have much else to do—but on the whole he left whatever leisurely figuring-out of situations might be necessary to the more analytical Doc. In a situation such as this, that was a definite advantage. Raider moved almost before he himself realized he was moving. It was certainly a fraction of a second before Cristóbal realized it.

Raider's left hand snaked forward like the darting tongue of a fat, russet diamondback and deflected Cristóbal's right hand before it even reached the holster. At almost the same time he brought himself a step nearer the squat bandit and brought his knee up, swiftly and viciously, into his groin.

Cristóbal gave a retching gasp of pain. Raider followed immediately with a short, hooking blow of his right fist, catching Cristóbal on the side of his jaw. It was like hitting a thick column of granite. Cristóbal staggered a little but didn't go down.

Raised on a farm, Raider was familiar with dreary chores. Like chopping wood, for example. He knew that such chores were only finished by duffing into them and by continuing until they were done. Dropping Cristóbal had become such a chore; he would just have to be hit until the blows wore him down. Cristóbal was trying to strike back, but he wasn't very skillful at it, and most of his re-

41

turn blows were ineffective—wild clumsy swings Raider either managed to parry or evade easily. At any rate, because he was directing all his attention upon the task at hand, Raider didn't notice the swift approach of several other men who stepped from the nearby shadows where they'd been lurking—acting as sentinels for Cristóbal, as he realized later. His first awareness of their presence came as a rifle stock swished through the air, arching down from above and behind, barely missing his head and shoulder only because at that moment he had shifted position to draw back for a blow to Cristóbal's midriff.

Again without conscious thought, he whirled to meet this new danger. He caught a glimpse of the several forms—four or five, maybe—that were converging upon him. Almost before he could count properly, another rifle, held by the barrel like a club, slammed toward him and caught him on the top and side of the head, making a loud *crack!* that reverberated inside his skull and sent a shooting pain through the pulp of his back teeth. Dazed, Raider knew he was falling to his hands and knees, but he was unable to do anything to prevent it.

The daze held, as though his head had suddenly been encased in a block of calf's-foot jelly. Nothing was clear; there didn't seem to be a passage of time that could be marked by seconds—or maybe it was minutes. There was only a swirling series of kaleidoscopic impressions. He was on the ground. He was shaking his head at it. He was trying to will his arms and legs to move, but they wouldn't. Blows were coming from all sides. Kicks, mostly—the hard, blunt toes of jackboots. There was a sporadic chattering in Spanish as though the men kicking him were perhaps also cursing him in that language.

And then the block of jelly around him seemed to melt away, and he realized that there *had* been a passage of time during which the men had suddenly withdrawn and clattered off, though he hadn't the faintest idea why.

Doc's voice said, "You okay, Rade?" He looked up and saw Doc standing over him.

Back in the hotel room, Raider, with Doc's help, poured water from the big china pitcher on the washstand into the tin basin, and, with the washrag provided, daubed at some of his bruises.

"Feel better now?" asked Doc.

"Not too good. But better." The flickering of Raider's lips was something less than a grin.

"Good thing I came along."

"Yeah," said Raider. "I wondered about that."

"Just decided I wanted a little night air."

"Like hell, I'll bet," said Raider. "You got to thinkin' about it and decided to join me at Madame Valdez's after all."

"If you say so." Doc shrugged. "Anyway, what do you suppose those hombres were up to?"

"Pilfering the wagon, that's all," said Raider, squinting at himself in the mirror. He'd removed his shirt, and his lean muscles were rippling in the dim, yellow light of the coal-oil lamp. The pungent, almost metallic smell of its flame hung faintly in the air of the room.

"Not sure about that," said Doc, frowning. "You say this one that looks like a bullfrog came out of the wagon with a bottle of medicine in his hand."

"About all he could find, I reckon."

"Which doesn't make sense. If he was pilfering he was after something of value. He'd either take a lot of medicine, which maybe he could sell, or none at all."

"Maybe he thought it was whiskey."

"Could be. Likely he might not be able to read. But, again, why just one bottle? Unless it was just a whim. You know—as long as he was there, he figured, he might as well pick up a bottle, which likely wouldn't be missed."

"What in the hell are you getting at, Doc?"

"The odd way it all stacks up," Doc said. "One man forces the lock, pokes around in the wagon. The others stake out nearby, keep an eye open for him. But they didn't call out any warning when you came along. Of course, that could be because they wanted you to tangle with this Cristóbal first, so they'd have the drop on you, good and proper."

"Doc," said Raider, drawing away from the mirror and pouring himself a glass of drinking water, "you're makin' more out of this than there is."

"Maybe," said Doc. "But the way it looks to me, they weren't there to steal anything valuable. Common sense'd tell 'em we wouldn't leave anything like that in the wagon. What they were doing, I'm thinking, is trying to get a line on us. Find papers or something that'd tell them who we really are and why we're really here."

"You just said Cristóbal probably couldn't read."

"That's right. So he wasn't doing it for himself but for someone else."

Raider's eyebrows cocked upward slightly. "Somebody like Magrue maybe?"

"Wouldn't put it past him," said Doc.

Raider was thoughtful for a moment. "Well, it looks like we're dealin' with somebody not only powerful in these parts but kind of tricky. We'll just have to be on our toes from now on."

"That," said Doc, nodding, "is *mainly* what I was getting at."

*   *   *

By mid-morning the sun was already bright upon the ocher dust of the land, making sharp purple shadows to the west of everything. Raider and Doc had set up the medicine wagon on the main street, near the corner of the plaza. The tailgate, dropped and supported by two barrels, made a kind of platform, and they stood upon it, behind a table they'd unfolded on which stood samples of the various medicines they were offering for sale.

Raider had put on a shirt embroidered with roses, and Doc, a step behind and to one side of him, was in a pearl-gray ensemble, complete with derby and a flowing ascot tie in the center of which reposed a huge fake ruby stickpin. He was plucking away at his five-string banjo and, in a pleasant though not particularly marvelous voice, rendering a chorus of "Fruit o' the Hangin' Tree," which was popular back east right now and which he'd managed to pick up on his last visit to Chicago.

> "They hung him early in the morn,
>   The townfolk came to see;
>   They left his widow all forlorn,
>   Pickin' fruit from the Hangin' Tree...."

There was already a crowd of thirty or so people around the wagon, attracted by the music, and as the song trailed off, Raider stepped down into it to collect money from those who would presumably buy medicine before long, while Doc, smiling, set his banjo down and stepped forward to deliver his spiel.

He held a bottle in his hand, showing it to everyone. "Now, folks, I can see that all of you here in Tesqua are real fine people, deserving of the best, but not always getting it 'cause you're so far off the beaten track! I will tell you, folks, the world of scientific medicine is coming up these days with marvels you just wouldn't believe! These are ordinarily reserved for folks in the big cities, but my colleague, Mr. Raider, who is a distinguished businessman, and I have decided to bring them out here to the folks who really deserve them!"

At the far edge of the crowd one nervous youth sounded a loud guffaw, apparently meant to express doubt.

Doc pointed at him immediately. "Yes," he said. "We've even got medicines that'll quiet down braying jackasses!"

The crowd laughed, and Doc knew that they were with him.

"Now, here in my hand at this very moment," Doc resumed, holding up the bottle again, "is the latest miracle of modern science, which I myself have perfected after many experiments and travel to far countries, including sunny Spain. I will have to ask the ladies in this fine gathering to bear with me now, and not to blush, for I am about to touch on somewhat delicate matters."

Some of the ladies shifted where they stood and looked at each other briefly.

"It is a fact, ladies—and gentlemen, too—a fact and a sad one, that at times the ardor of a husband and wife may be dampened. And when it disappears, love often flies out the window. Well, the latest scientific researches into this have shown that it need not be!" He waved the bottle and pointed to its label. "Dr. Weatherbee's Elixir del Amor," he said. "Guaranteed to arouse passion in the coldest of hearts. I cannot reveal its entire medical formula, naturally, but I can tell you this much. The main ingredient is a rare Spanish beetle, known as the cantharis, which is dried and ground and provides the affectionate urge in man, woman, or beast. It can be used to encourage the breeding of fine stock, or, if you desire, to restore amorous relationships between those whom the good Lord has blessed with wedlock."

Doc's warning notwithstanding, several of the ladies in the crowd were indeed blushing as they glanced at each other. And some of the men were grinning a touch salaciously.

"But Elixir del Amor," Doc continued, "is more than an aphrodisiac, which is what concoctions to restore passion are called in scientific circles. I have added to it my own secret formula of a restorative tonic, so that the necessary energy is imparted to those who find themselves with renewed desire. Take as directed, and even those of you who have reached the golden years will find new pleasures in your daily or, if I may say so, in your *hourly* lives! I am certain that all of you, who are intelligent adults, understand my meaning."

He paused to let that much sink in.

"I must remind you," said Doc, "that Elixir del Amor can be sold only to husbands and wives, since my associate and I do not condone adultery or any other form of sin. And since I see nothing but honest faces out there before me this morning, I will accept the word of each one of you that you wish to purchase this elixir only for moral purposes and not for seduction."

The price of this sovereign remedy, as Doc announced it, was not ten dollars, not five, not even one dollar, but a mere two bits, and, when he had finished his pitch, Raider began to collect the quarters and pass out the bottles. Most of the purchasers were men—some grinning, a few looking shy. The usual explanation was that it was for the person's breeding stock or favorite dogs. Within a short time they had sold enough to make a modest profit and to decide that male-female relationships in Tesqua were definitely in need of some kind of improvement.

They were shutting the wagon so that it could be returned to its parking place by the livery stable when the tall, white-haired, aristocratic-looking hidalgo who had spoken to them the day before approached and greeted them with the suggestion of a bow.

"Señores," he said, courteously, almost ceremoniously.

"Don Luis," said Doc, returning his nod.

"I trust you found your accommodations comfortable and that you are enjoying your stay here in Tesqua."

"Everything's first-rate," said Raider, examining the handsome old man quietly, knowing very well he had something other than that inquiry on his mind. "Better than lots of places we've been."

"Evidently you travel extensively."

"Some," said Raider, nodding, understating it.

"I, too, have seen some of the outside world," said Don Luis. "But that was when I was younger and had both more reason and opportunity to travel. It is more comfortable now to remain in my *quinto* and, in an old man's way, I suppose, to dream of past glories. At any rate, I know that there are many exciting developments in the centers of civilization that never reach us here in Tesqua. This, uh, elíxir of yours, for example. I am most curious about it."

"Well," said Doc, chiming in, "it's a scientific marvel, all right. Not much doubt of that."

"Truly? You will forgive me, but there is the possibility that it is not as effective as you claim. Or even that it might have other, harmful effects."

"Don Luis," said Doc, "I give you my word of honor that Elixir del Amor contains nothing that will disturb a patient's good health in the slightest."

"Yup. That's the truth," said Raider. And it was. Colored water, a little sugar, and a few drops of grain alcohol never hurt anyone, as far as he knew.

"You can understand, I hope, that I must be cautious," said Don Luis. He smiled a little. "I haven't many years left and I would prefer that they pass with as few difficulties as possible. My mind would be at ease if I knew more about this medicine of yours before I, uh, tried it."

"Well," said Doc, "the formula's kind of scientific. It can't be explained easily to anyone outside the profession."

"Would you nevertheless take the time to do so?" asked Don Luis.

"I'd be honored," said Doc, making the little half bow Don Luis had started again. "Set a spell, and I'll go over it for you."

"I've a better idea," said Don Luis. "Perhaps you gentlemen would care to join me for the midday meal at my *quinto*. We can discuss the matter at our leisure."

"Doubly honored," said Doc, with yet another bow.

After giving them directions to his house, which was a little beyond the town, Don Luis departed and Doc and Raider continued with their chore of buttoning up the wagon and parking it. Presently they were riding side by side along the winding road that led, gently rising, toward the foothills just east of the settlement.

Raider had been thoughtful ever since they'd spoken to Don Luis Mondragon. He glanced at Doc now. "What do you think?"

"About what?"

"This Don Luis. What do you think he's really got on his mind?"

"Hard to say," said Doc. "Could be it's only the elixir. It's likely enough the old fellow can't get it up as often as he'd like."

"In that case the tonic ain't gonna do him much good," said Raider.

"On the contrary," Doc said. "If a person takes real Spanish fly all it does is kind of burn hell out of his pecker, though that'll make a bull horny so he'll breed. But with some folks this elixir of mine actually works like I say it does. I've seen it happen. Not so much the medicine as their belief in it. They expect it to stimulate them, and so, by God, it does."

"Could be." Raider shrugged a little. "Anyway, all we can do is play along and find out what ideas he's got, if any. Fact is, we might learn even more about the setup here from Don Luis. So I guess we're not wastin' our time seein' him."

"Exactly the way I was looking at it," said Doc, nodding.

They continued riding, keeping their horses at a walk. The sun was high now, and the purple shadows were directly below the stolid cottonwoods that lined the road. There was a lazy silence all about, broken only by the occasional barking of a dog or the clucking of scrawny chickens in the scattered *jacales* they passed. For most of the denizens of Tesqua and its environs it was now siesta time.

CHAPTER FIVE

The estate of Don Luis Mondragon was entered by a gateway at the road, where a huge crossbeam atop wooden pillars bore the carved letters of his family name. A driveway marked by tall poplars on either side led to the house, a low, rambling adobe structure with the usual *vigas* protruding from its walls just below roof level. A covered well stood in the clearing in front of its main entrance.

Servants in loose cotton garments emerged to greet Raider and Doc and take their horses. As they walked to the front door, Raider said, "What was it he called this place? His *quinto*?"

"About the same as hacienda," said Doc. "It means a fifth part—the way estates are divided when they're passed on to the various heirs."

Raider grinned a little. "Don't you get tired sometimes holdin' all those things you keep in your head?"

"You never know what's gonna be useful sometime," said Doc, shrugging.

Oaken doors swung open and they were led into a large vestibule. Serapes and Navaho blankets hung on the walls as decoration. The thick adobe walls made it much cooler here than in the hot sun outside.

Almost immediately, as they entered, a young woman came through one of the portals leading to the vestibule and stepped toward them, smiling. She was dressed, as Don Luis had been, in an embroidered suit with tight trousers, a bright red sash, and a vestlike jacket, but it was her face, with its exquisitely proportioned features, that drew their attention. Her skin had the color of fine desert sand, and her lips were broad, red satin ribbons. Her large dark eyes were faintly slanted, with an almost Oriental cast. She was small, but in the way she held herself, with her tiny shoulders proudly squared, she seemed to be taller.

"Grato, señores," she said, in a low, silken voice. "I am Susanita."

Doc essayed the little bow he seemed to have picked up from Don Luis.

Raider grinned and said, "Howdy, ma'am."

"Don Luis is busy at the moment and asked me to greet you. He will join you presently."

"I didn't know he had such a beautiful daughter," said Doc.

"I am not his daughter." Susanita's smile switched slightly, like a horse's tail brushing at flies. "I am his wife."

"Oh," said Doc—and there wasn't much else he could say.

She led them to a room where there was a large dining table already covered with dishes, bowls of fruit, and decanters of wine. As they found chairs there—Susanita taking one at the head of the table—Doc noticed that she directed most of her glances toward Raider, and saw what he thought was definite interest in her eyes. He was mildly disappointed at that, but consoled himself with the thought that Genevieve Ashley had cottoned to him rather than to his partner. There was a mystery to the way certain people found immediate attraction to certain others, and he never really had gotten to the bottom of it.

Susanita poured wine for them, and a small quantity into her own glass. It tasted a mite sweet to Raider, but it did warm his throat a bit as it went down.

"Don Luis tells me that you are strangers to Tesqua, and that you've come here to sell medicines of various kinds."

"That's right, ma'am," said Raider, his eyes fastened upon her so hard that Doc figured he was scarcely hearing himself talk. "We travel all around doin' that, but this is the first time we've hit these parts. I can see we should have come here long before this. There sure is a lot that's beautiful to look at around here."

"Yes," said Susanita. "There is much beauty here. And it is quite peaceful. Perhaps too peaceful. Perhaps, at times, too quiet."

"Well, I can see there's not too much excitement," Raider said. "Especially for a lovely young woman who might fit better someplace where there's a lot of social affairs and things goin' on."

"I cannot complain." There was a touch of astringency to her smile. "It is true that there is more activity in Santa Fe, where I was born and raised. But I made my choice when I married Don Luis and came here. I will confess, señores, that my circumstances were less comfortable before than they are now. And I must say that Don Luis is very gracious, very kind."

"Glad to hear you found what you want," said Raider. "That is, if you really have."

Doc, somewhat amused, watched the unspoken words sparkle back and forth between Raider's and Susanita's eyes. It was his guess they'd just about forgotten he was here and were half imagining themselves to be alone.

They were still looking at each other like that when Don Luis himself entered the room. If he noticed the way they were locking eyes, he didn't let on. He murmured a greeting to Raider and Doc, took a chair, and glanced at Susanita, who smiled, excused herself, and left. A moment later a servant —an older man in loose white clothes—entered with a tray of food he set upon the table.

"Now, then, gentlemen," said Don Luis, when they had begun to eat, "I suspect you already have an idea as to what my little problem is. We are men of the world, and I trust we can discuss this frankly and with proper understanding. You have met Susanita. What do you think of her?"

"Mighty pretty," said Raider, noncommittally.

"Yes. And, as you might assume, a very passionate woman. I do not mean to be indiscreet, but this is necessary to our discussion. I was quite lonely when my former wife died, and when I met Susanita in Santa Fe I was immediately struck by her beauty. I do not deceive myself, however. She cannot possibly feel for me the love she might have for a younger and, uh, more vigorous man. She married me for the wealth and security I could give her, and we both openly acknowledge this arrangement to each other. As long as I am being candid, I will carry it all the way. Observing Susanita's manner and bearing, would you not say that she is a woman of breeding?"

"And then some, I'd say," answered Raider.

"The truth of the matter is somewhat different." Don Luis delicately patted his sweeping white mustaches with a linen napkin. "Not that I found her in a cantina or a house of pleasures, such as Madame Valdez's place here in Tesqua. A degree or two above that, at least. One required an appointment with Susanita and one had to be well-off to afford her favors. I'm sorry to say that some of the old biddies here have learned of her background and are less than friendly toward her. This, of course, only increases her loneliness."

"Looks like you *have* got a problem, Don Luis," Doc said sympathetically.

The old man nodded. "It is why I'm interested in this tonic of yours, or whatever it is. I find it hard to believe that it does all you say it will, but I turn to it, I suppose, in desperation. I have tried everything else, even oysters, which I once sent for all the way from San Francisco. They spoiled before they ever got here. I brought a *kurau* here—a medicine man—to do his chants and wave his sacred pouch, in the hope that there might be something to this Indian magic, but that didn't seem to work, either. In short, señores, I'm willing to try anything, no matter how farfetched it seems."

"I can understand how you'd go to a lot of trouble to keep somebody like Susanita happy," Raider said.

"It is more than merely keeping her happy," replied Don Luis. "It is to keep her from leaving me, which I do not think I could bear."

"I'll have to be honest with you, too," Doc interjected. "I've seen the elixir work for some people, but there's no absolute guarantee as to what it'll do. All I can say is that it won't hurt you if you try it."

"Is there any special way in which it should be taken? Perhaps to increase its effectiveness—"

"Well, I'll give you full instructions before we leave, Don Luis. And a bottle of the stuff with our compliments. But as long as we're here I'd like to ask you a few questions about these parts. Mr. Raider here, and myself, figured we might stick around awhile, since it is such nice country, providing we can do enough business to make it worthwhile. I might add that I'm also a veterinarian,

and it strikes me there might be a need for my
services with some of the ranchers and farmers in
the area. Unfortunately, we have reason to believe
we might not be exactly welcome in certain quarters."

Don Luis smiled faintly. "You must be thinking
of Seth Magrue."

Doc's eyebrows rose. "How did you know?"

"If there's trouble, Señor Magrue is probably behind it," said Don Luis, shrugging. "How he moved
in here and gained control is such a long story that
I haven't time to tell it all now. But he and his col-
leagues *do* run the town—and that's what we're
concerned with. I mean no insult to you, personally, when I say that they are all Anglos, and that this
land really belongs to us of Spanish descent who
have been settled here for more than three centuries. I think there would be no quarrel between
the Anglos and the Spanish if Magrue did not
make it. But, as it's happened, the men he picks
hold all the important offices and dictate what is to
be done. You can be sure that they manipulate
things so that we Spanish pay most of the taxes
and are often forced to relinquish land and water
rights and other valuable considerations. If it goes
on like this, Magrue and his associates will even-
tually own everything."

"Well, why don't you just vote Magrue's men
out of office?" asked Raider.

"Easier said than done," Don Luis replied. "Our
people are inclined to be—how shall I say it?—not
lazy, but with a sense of letting things go. We had
a different form of government before the Anglos
came, and they are not used to voting or exercising
democracy in other ways. It is worse than that.
They have lost, in recent years, much of their tra-
dition, much of their pride. I've done what little I

could to perhaps restore it. The festival yesterday
—I was active on the committee that arranged it.
As for politics, well, there's a small group of us
trying to get my nephew elected to the sheriff's
post next election. If we can persuade enough people to vote he may be able to replace Sheriff Busby,
who is Magrue's man. But most of them are un-
interested, and some are afraid. Magrue's people
have made veiled threats." He smiled a little. "Perhaps I shouldn't be telling you all this, but you
said Magrue didn't seem to be making you welcome, so I assume you're not also on his side. At
least not yet."

"The way things look, I don't expect we'll ever
be," said Raider, leaning back in his chair and
glancing at the portal as though half hoping Susanita might show herself there again. "And it's
not only us Magrue seems to be rubbing the wrong
way—unless I'm seeing it all wrong. I heard he
wasn't inclined to do much for Professor Ashley
and his daughter."

"Ah, yes—those two. They came here in your
company, I understand. The professor has some
kind of interest in the Indian pueblos, does he
not?"

"He's looking for old artifacts from the time of
Coronado," Doc explained. "Very important his-
torically, the way he tells it."

Don Luis frowned into the air for a moment. "I
may be able to help the professor. I have family
records dating back to those times that might be of
interest to him. In fact, it might help with this
sense of pride among our people I mentioned before—knowing that some of their history is being
taken seriously by scholars." He pushed himself
back from the table abruptly and rose. "Well, gen-

tlemen, if you can leave this tonic of yours and give me whatever instruction is necessary—"

"Be glad to," said Raider. "Anything we can do to keep a lovely lady happy."

Shortly afterward, Doc and Raider emerged again into the bright sun and servents brought their horses to them. They mounted and waved to Don Luis, who stood in the doorway. As they turned to ride off, Raider noticed the little folded piece of paper wedged into his saddle just below the applehorn. He reached for it and opened it with one hand, keeping it down near the saddle as be read it. The handwriting was feminine yet bold, unhesitating.

The mission at Ranchitos. Midnight.

There was no signature. The slight redolence of musky perfume, when Raider lifted the refolded note to his nostrils, was signature enough.

Doc and Raider spent the rest of the afternoon at the dreary but necessary task of manufacturing a new batch of Elixir del Amor. They had the bottles for it, and the labels, printed in Denver, and also the caramel coloring, but the water, sugar, and alcohol, which would have been too weighty in the wagon, had to be procured anew. The sugar was obtained in the Martinez Grocery and General Store on the plaza, but they had to drive the wagon to the Taos Lightning Distillery beyond the edge of town to get the grain alcohol. Mixing, pouring, pasting labels, kept them busy till near suppertime.

At the hotel, the management seemed surprised to hear they wanted another bath, after having taken one just yesterday, but finally sent servants with the galvanized tub and buckets of hot water. Throughout all of this, Raider was untalkative, and Doc knew he had something on his mind. Politely, he didn't ask what. When he saw Raider secretly consulting a small, folded note several times, he kind of guessed what it might be, anyway.

Dressed and refreshed, they entered the dining room just past sundown. Almost immediately they saw Professor Ashley and Genevieve at one of the tables, and, having seen them, they wandered that way. The professor rose and urged them to join him and his daughter for dinner. Doc and Raider accepted gladly and sat down at the table.

"Well, how are your researches coming along?" asked Doc. He was addressing both of them, but his eyes were spending most of the time on Genevieve. She looked remarkably civilized and a little out of place in a pale blue silk dress with puffs at the sleeves.

"Not as well as I'd expected, I'm afraid," said the professor. "I spent the day at the main church, digging into old records, but without much result, though the fathers there were very kind. They travel out to the pueblos, you know, to minister to their Indian communicants, most of whom are at least nominal Christians, though they continue to practice many of their own religious ways."

Raider looked up. "Don't suppose you got to someplace called the Ranchitos mission, did you?"

"No, I didn't. I believe that's an abandoned mission south of town. Why do you ask?"

"Heard about the place. Just curious," said Raider, shrugging.

"The problem, you see," said Genevieve, who hadn't listened closely to that exchange, "is one of time. We're sure the artifacts are in *one* of the pueblos, but we're not sure which. We could visit them one by one, I suppose, but that would mean miles and miles of riding, to say nothing of the time spent at each one to gain the confidence of the Indians. The entire summer might be gone before we made any progress."

Doc looked thoughtful. "Don Luis Mondragon might help," he said. "He's one of the old-line hidalgos around here—Raider and I saw him on business today. He said he had some family records that might have the kind of information you're looking for."

"Oh?" Genevieve's eyebrows rose. "Family records can be very fruitful. How do we get in touch with this Don Luis?"

"Don't believe he'd mind if we called on him this evening," said Doc. "It's just a short ride out to his *quinto*. Raider and I will go along, if you like, and introduce you to him."

"Make it just yourself, Doc," said Raider. "I got a few things to do."

"Okay. Just me." Doc shrugged. He looked at Genevieve again. "Want to do that?"

"You're very kind to us," said Genevieve. "Yes, we'd love to meet Don Luis and see his records."

"Then afterward, maybe," said Doc, his eyes switching back and forth between the professor and his daughter, "the professor here could go back and study them, and you and I could take a little stroll in the cool night air."

Her smile, turned upon Doc, said all she couldn't say aloud. "Yes. A little stroll." She turned to her father abruptly. "You wouldn't mind, would you, Father?"

"What?" He looked up. "Oh, yes. An evening stroll. You go ahead, Genevieve. If we get any records, I'll want to study them right away."

"Good," said Doc. "Looks like the evening's all set."

"Sure does," said Raider, showing the slight relaxation of his lips that was his version of a secret smile.

At the hacienda, Don Luis seemed surprised to see Doc again so soon, but graciously admitted everyone as soon as Doc explained why he'd brought Professor Ashley and his daughter. He took them into the library, called for wine, and began to open a series of huge old ledgers, bound in cracked and dusty leather. Doc and Genevieve sat together in a corner of the room and quickly and surreptitiously felt various places on each other's bodies as the two old men pored over the records, murmuring to each other whenever they found items of interest. Several times, when Genevieve stroked Doc's huge, now-hardened knuckle through the fabric of his trousers, giggling softly as she did so, Doc had all he could do to keep from tearing her clothes off and laying her then and there, the others in the room be damned. The way they were concentrating on those ledgers he just about might have been able to do it unnoticed.

Both men white-haired and slender, Professor Ashley and Don Luis faintly resembled each other. Ashley, with his unkempt hair and rumpled clothes, was less organized and self-contained, while Don Luis, with his sweeping white mustaches, was considerably more suave and polished. But the way each threw himself wholeheartedly into the task at hand was much the same, and it was clear to Doc and Genevieve that they had cottoned to each other from the moment they'd met.

"*Pues!* Look what we have here!" said Don Luis at one point, as they bent over one of the opened books. "My ancestor—Porfirio Mondragon y Villaseñor. It is a kind of log of his activities he kept.

On this date, it says, he visited the pueblo at Spanish Rock. And a note. Many riches there, in a secret place! What do you think of that?"

"That's the Zama Pueblo," said Ashley, nodding. "I always rather favored it. And riches in a secret place. Yes, that fits admirably. Just think, Don Luis, the very objects Coronado's men used in their daily lives—the very ones they held and touched centuries ago!"

"But he says riches—*riqueza* in Spanish."

"Of course. And riches they are—riches beyond price."

"You do not understand. In our usage, *riquezas* would not mean objects of, let us say, historical value. Only actual riches. Treasures. Gold, silver, jewels—that sort of thing."

Professor Ashley frowned. "Well, from everything I've looked into so far I didn't expect anything like that. Oh, I suppose there might be some precious metal, but nothing in the way of a fortune."

"Even so, you could undoubtedly use riches of that kind. We all could. I am quite comfortable, financially, as far as my personal affairs are concerned, but I haven't nearly enough to pay for the election campaign we need to drive Magrue and his people out of office."

"In that case," said Ashley, turning to smile at the old hidalgo, "if we find any *riquezas,* as you call them, they are yours, and for a good cause, I will say."

"You are more than generous, señor!" said Don Luis.

Overhearing this, Genevieve took her hand from Doc's thigh. "More than generous, indeed! Downright impractical! Father, you really must stop giving away everything, the way you do!"

"We will discuss business details later, my dear," said Ashley, a dreamy look in his eyes. "And now, Don Luis, let's continue with these marvelous records of yours and see what else we can find."

Raider approached the old mission at Ranchitos cautiously, not because he expected any specific trouble, but because it had become his habit to approach any place cautiously, especially at night. The habit was so ingrained by now that it was almost an instinct—one he shared with such creatures as the mountain lion and the bobcat. He rode at a walk, his own wariness somehow transmitting itself to the claybank mare, which took care not to clatter too much with its hooves on the hard, dry ground.

The mission ahead, with its adobe walls silver-bellied in the moonlight, seemed to grow from that hard, dry ground rather than to squat in place upon it. The adobe was splotched and crumbled in places; one of the bell towers at the front of the structure looked half chopped away. Its few small window apertures were dark and lifeless, like eye sockets in a sun-bleached skull. There were missions like this one all over the countryside in this region, and why it had been abandoned Raider didn't know and didn't care. If it had been other than a mission, he supposed, with a certain sanctity in its past, someone without a home would have moved into it.

He rode a broad circle around the structure before dismounting. On the other side of it he saw a small black horse, its reins on a lopsided hitching rail—Susanita's horse, if all was well. He overheaded the reins of his mare, finally, and swung himself down from the saddle.

She was in the shadow of the mission's broad

front entrance. As he stepped toward it, she came forward a little, into the moonlight. She wore what he now supposed must be her usual garb: tight Spanish trousers, a broad sash, a vestlike jacket, richly embroidered. The moon made pale ivory of her skin; ivory without a blemish.

Her eyes cat-tailed as she looked up at him. He paused before her. He sensed that she felt as he did: that in this moment there was nothing that needed to be said. She swayed toward him almost imperceptibly, and, with that, Raider took her into his arms and lowered a kiss on her broad red lips, which parted slightly to receive it. Not a passionate kiss yet—that was for later. This was introductory; a foreshadowing. Raider had never concerned himself much with art, but it had to be admitted there was a certain art, a certain finesse, as Doc probably would have said, to this kind of thing. The moist, velvet feel of her lips started his blood singing; he swore he could feel it coursing more swiftly through his veins..

Silently, Susanita took his hand, turned gracefully, and led him into the interior of the mission. Shafts of moonlight came through the window apertures, and, as his eyes became used to the dimmer light, he saw that she was taking him toward a long *banco* that lay like an adobe bench along the foot of one wall.

The motions that go into the act of undressing, Raider reflected, can get kind of clumsy-looking; it usually made him impatient to wait for a woman to strip if it happened to be necessary. But Susanita, he now saw, made a kind of dance out of it. It was as though guitars strummed and castanets clicked in an arrogant flamenco. Her vest removed, she placed the end of her sash in his hand and spun away from him, unwinding it; her trousers fell, and she stepped from them lightly: then, approaching him again, she slipped out of her blouse and, presently, the rest of her light undergarments.

She stood before him, shoulders squared, chin high, her dark eyes meeting his squarely, somehow defiantly. Her breasts, well shaped and firm, were upright, pouting at him. Her pose, in some odd Castilian way, dared him to give her pleasure—if he was capable of it.

Watching all this, Raider scarcely remembered shucking his own duds, but he must have done that, for now he, too, was naked before her. His whip-handle dong rose at a sharp angle, all but bursting from the pressure within it, and he saw that Susanita was unable to control a flickering glance of surprise at the size of it.

He crushed her to him suddenly and roughly, pressing his member to her flat belly and the large triangular patch of dark hair at the base of it. With dancelike motions, they rubbed against each other, massaging Raider's huge member as it stood upright, caught between them. Susanita, clutching his penis in her hand, eased Raider, still pressed tightly against her, to the long *banco* at the foot of the wall, until both were stretched out upon it, Raider on top.

She embraced him with her thighs and he thrust himself into her. His member sank swiftly into the lubricated cavern in that thick patch of dark hair. She made her first real sound since he had met her at the mission door—a gasp of delight that had a touch of pain in it.

"Lentemente, querido!" she murmured.

Raider, pumping away, grinned slightly. "Slowly, huh? Don't worry, gal. Somethin' this good's gotta last awhile."

As the uncounted minutes passed, the tempo of Raider's thrustings, and her pelvic responses to meet them, increased, and their flamenco dance rose wildly toward its climax. When at last he poured himself into her she was clinging to him so tightly that their flesh—Raider's hard marble, hers smooth ivory—was melded together into what seemed one substance. The inner explosion that followed was, for both of them, a bursting shower of stars.

She was silent, with her eyes tightly closed, as Raider at last withdrew gently. Her firm breasts with their maroon nipples rose and fell with her breathing. Then she opened her eyes slowly, looked at Raider still half crouched over her, and said, "You are not finished, are you?"

"Not by a damn sight," he said. "Lots more where that came from."

It was the better part of an hour before both were surfeited—though even this, both knew, was temporary; if they rested long enough they'd be at it again with a joyful hunger neither could resist. They'd brought about each climax with different positions, and there was, in both, the unspoken feeling that they had by no means exhausted all the possible variations. Raider was pleased. Susanita, as he now discovered, was more than pleased.

"Raider—" She was naked and still beside him, running her fingers lightly up and down the hair of his torso.

"Yeah?"

"It has never been like this for me."

"Well . . . it's always kinda different," he said.

"I mean I have had many men. I will not deny this. But I think we . . . you and I . . . do well together. Do you not think we have found something wonderful?"

"Well," said Raider cautiously, "it was fine for me. Right fine."

She turned her head toward him abruptly. "Raider, *querido,*" she said intensely, "I thought to be with Don Luis, who gives me everything I wish— except what you can give—was what I wanted. Now I think I was mistaken. Take me with you, Raider! I do not care where we go—just take me with you!"

It took Raider a frowning moment to answer. "You're some gal, Susanita—hardly anybody else like you—but somethin' like that just wouldn't work out for either of us."

"You do not care for me, then!" Her eyes flashed.

"Ain't that. If you mean love, though, that always leads to the preacher, and I don't think that's in me. Not yet, anyway. But with you, somethin' close to it maybe. Just the same, there's your life, and my life, which you don't even know about, and the two just wouldn't go together."

"There is another woman?"

"Nobody in particular," said Raider dryly.

"Then what is to stand in the way?"

"Lots," he said. "Can't explain it. You'll just have to take my word for it."

"I am nothing but a toy. To use and throw away!" she said with sudden anger.

"No, it ain't that way either."

She would not be mollified. She slipped away from him, rose, and began to put her clothes on again. "I could say it in Spanish, Raider," she said. "But there is an Anglo expression that is better." She paused and stared at him. "I hate your guts, Raider!"

"Oh, come on now," Raider said, rising from the *banco*.

"Do not come near me! You will be sorry, Raider. That I can promise you."

"Doggone it, gal—"

"Enough!" She tucked the final winding of her sash into place. "You do not know me, Raider; you do not know what pride is in my blood. Yes . . . you will be sorry!"

"If you'd just look at this here thing with some common sense—" Raider began.

She pirouetted toward the door. "Good night, Señor Raider!" she said. *"Hasta la vista!* And I'm sure I will see you again. You can count on it."

Raider sighed to himself a number of times as he got dressed again. Sighed and shook his head. He'd figured out a lot of the mysteries of the big sky, the sweeping plains, and the shining mountains, but women—well, that was a different story. In a way, he was glad that there was still lots to be done about Seth Magrue and the situation he and Doc had come to investigate here in Tesqua. Keeping busy would take his mind off wondering what in hell was going on in Susanita's pretty head— and why.

CHAPTER SIX

"And this latest scientific discovery," said Doc, holding up a bottle of Elixir del Amor, as he stood on the tailgate of the medicine wagon, "is a great benefit to mankind, folks, restoring bliss and happiness to those blessed in holy wedlock!"

Raider, below him, ready to pass through the crowd with bottles and collect money, glanced up at him sardonically, certain that no one would notice. The crowd was new; the wagon was halted in one of the small outlying settlements perhaps an hour's ride from Tesqua. Neither Raider nor Doc had particularly wanted to go out and peddle the elixir again, but they had a masquerade to sustain and knew it might look suspicious if they didn't continue acting like purveyors of medicine.

Doc was busy with his spiel, and it was Raider who first noticed that the crowd gathered around the wagon was not quite the ordinary crowd they might have expected. Hard to say what alarmed him in the beginning—a sixth sense, possibly, though Raider never thought much about mystical things like that. The earliest sensation was just one of being bothered; something not right; something out of kilter. What was it? Nothing in the main part of the crowd, nearest the wagon— something out along the edge of the crowd. Persons out there that just didn't fit somehow. He frowned, rose on tiptoe, and peered more intently in that direction.

Take that lean, hollow-eyed hombre in a kind of lounging pose off to one side. Holding himself a little too stiff for someone who was supposed to be lounging. Hogleg on his thigh, strapped down for drawing, if need be. And on the other flank a smaller man with a mirthless half grin that showed most of his teeth missing. Likewise armed. In the center a full-bearded man in faded old army trousers standing, like a soldier, at parade rest. *His* holster on the left and turned around for a cross draw. Anyway, armed, like the other two.

One thing was pretty sure. These three men, whoever they were, hadn't come here to stock up on Doc Weatherbee's miraculous Elixir del Amor.

Doc had now reached the part of his spiel where he was assuring the crowd he'd take anybody's word the elixir wouldn't be used for immoral purposes.

"Wrap it up, Doc," said Raider, interrupting quietly. "Trouble out there."

Doc picked up the cue immediately. "Be right back, folks! Don't go 'way!" He ducked into the wagon and emerged again, a few seconds later, strapping his Diamondback to his waist, jumping down from the tailgate to Raider's side. "I saw 'em, too," he whispered. "Who the hell are they?"

"Don't matter," said Raider, clipping off the words. "Way they look is what counts. What we do is move off easy now. Like we was maybe fetchin' something. Get the wagon between them and us."

"Just what I was thinkin'," said Doc, and Raider glanced at him to show his doubt that Doc had just been thinking that.

They strolled as though completely unalarmed to the front of the wagon, which had its whiffletrees on barrels so that Judith, who was tethered at a hitching rail in front of a cantina across the street, along with their horses, wouldn't decide to wander off with it in the middle of Doc's medicine pitch.

In a moment they were out of sight of the men on the edge of the crowd who had aroused Raider's suspicions. They were about to turn, draw their weapons, and peer back around the edge of the wagon, when, a short distance ahead of them, an immensely fat man stepped from the darkened doorway of the cantina, held a pistol pointed at them, and said, "Gents, make like you was made of ice and don't move so much as a whisker, either of you."

The fat man's smile made dimples in his fair, almost beardless cheeks. His eyes, though small, were as clear and blue as a baby's. His voluminous trousers—probably specially made to fit his immense girth—were held up by broad, red suspenders, and affixed to the left suspender, halfway to his shoulder, was a sheriff's star.

Raider stared at him for a moment, then said, "You must be Busby."

"*Sheriff* Busby," said the fat man, holding his dimpled smile, which, because of the hardness of his eyes, wasn't at all merry. "The title goes with the office, and I like to hear it. Now, you look like a couple of gents who's got their wits about them. So you must know there's deputies comin' up behind you and me, here, right in front of you. Seein' how all that is, smartest thing for you to do is unbuckle those gunbelts of yours and let 'em drop. Real slow and easy; no tricks. And pronto, if you don't mind."

Raider glanced at Doc. Doc shrugged faintly, and Raider nodded. Both men unbuckled and dropped their gunbelts. Doc said, "All right, Busby. *Sheriff* Busby. What's the charge, if any?"

"Hoosegow lawyers, huh? Figured you two would be. Well, there's a charge, all right. Violation of county ordinance eighty-three dash seven, peddlin'

without a license. And forty-two dash five, sellin'
liquor without a license. And don't tell me that
medicine of yours ain't liquor. One o' my deputies
got half drunk just tastin' it. Anyway, all that's up
to the judge. He ain't available now, so we're holdin' you till he is."

"Without bail on a misdemeanor?" said Doc,
angry, surprised.

Busby grinned, deepening his dimples. "Take it
to the Supreme Court if you want. Meanwhile,
you're goin' in the jug, both of you."

As Doc and Raider glared back at the sheriff, he
tucked his pistol under his arm, took a paper sack
from his pocket, poured some seedlike nuts into his
palm, and popped them into his mouth.

"Pinyon nuts," he said pleasantly. "Ever try
'em?"

"Come on, Busby," said Doc. "What's all this
really about?"

"On your horses," said Busby, his voice hard,
even though he appeared to be smiling. "You'll
have time to talk later. Plenty of it."

The county jail was combined with the sheriff's
office in one end of the low courthouse building on
the plaza. It consisted of two cells, open to the rest
of the room where Busby had a rolltop desk against
one wall. After the sheriff and his deputies herded
Doc and Raider into a cell, Busby dismissed the
others, leaned back in his swivel chair, put the
open sack of pinyon nuts on his desk and
munched on them as he held forth, facing his prisoners.

"Best thing they got around here, these pinyon
nuts," he said. "Can't say as I go for the enchiladas
and that kind of stuff. Don't hardly fill a man. Give
me steak and potatoes, I always say. What this

here town needs is an *American* restaurant with somebody who can make a decent apple pie. Now, if somebody would drift in here with somethin' like that in mind, he'd sure be a damn sight more welcome. Instead, all we get is real odd folks, with real odd ideas."

"Cut out beatin' around the bush, Busby," said Raider.

"Don't care for friendly conversation, is that it?" said Busby. "Well, if you want to make it hard on yourself that's up to you. You got it all wrong about this here jail of mine. We treat our prisoners right —even give 'em privileges when they cooperate. Like visitors. Yup. We got regular visiting hours."

"What's that got to do with us?" asked Raider.

"Now, you're not a very patient hombre, are you?" said Busby, stuffing his mouth with another handful of nuts. "Can't wait for a man to get to what he's got to say, so's he can say it proper. I was about to tell you there's a visitor on his way. You can have a nice chat with him, and that'll help you pass the time."

"All right, Busby," said Raider. "Who the hell is it?"

"You'll see," said the sheriff. He reached for a ledger book on his desk. "Meanwhile, got to book you. Don't care for the paperwork, myself, but it's got to be done. Gonna need your full names, includin' the middle, date o' birth, where you're from, why you're here, and things like that. And, by the way, don't refuse to give this here information. That violates another ordinance—up to thirty days, if I recall correctly."

Wearily, Raider and Doc answered the sheriff's questions, sticking to their cover stories as medicine men roaming the countryside, going wherever the whim of the moment dictated. They traded sarcastic smiles with Busby, smiles that said he didn't believe half of what they spoke, and also that they knew damn well he didn't believe them.

In the midst of this interrogation, the front door opened and a tall, bald man in garish dress stepped into the room. Doc and Raider immediately recognized Seth Magrue, whom they had seen talking to Genevieve in front of the courthouse. He appeared as though making a stage entrance, pausing at the doorway in a dramatic stance, as though taking in his surroundings, but also as though to let all present get a good look at him—and, of course, admire him. Some folks would admire that fancy getup of his, Doc supposed. His soft buckskin jacket, with all its fringes, looked new-made —not a smudge on it. Multicolored beadwork decorated it here and there. The motif was repeated in the band of his huge, cream-white Stetson. His belt buckle was silver and Navaho turquoise. An immense ring of the same materials was on his ring finger.

"Well, howdy, Seth!" said Busby. "Been waitin' for you."

Magrue nodded cursorily at the sheriff and kept his eyes on the prisoners. Studying him, Doc figured he must have been a handsome man in his youth—in a soft, bread-dough kind of way—and maybe still was, in a sense, in spite of some of the puffiness and heaviness to the jowls that had set in. He kept himself cleanly and closely shaven, and Doc thought he could smell the Bay Rum he used all the way across the room. "I've been waiting, too," he said finally. "I thought you two would have the good sense to come see me. Since you didn't, we'll just have to talk here."

Raider cocked his head quizzically. "Tell me, Magrue. Why would it have been good sense to come see you? There's a lot here I just don't figure out."

Magrue sighed—obviously for effect. "Let's get it straight right now, gentlemen. We're going to talk, and talk straight. Cards on the table. Don't try to pretend what isn't so, because I know most of what *is* so, and can find out the rest pretty quick. You know damned well who I am, and you know damned well nobody does anything in Tesqua without checking with me first. Now, as far as what I know, it's not so much knowing who you really are as knowing what you damn sure are not. One thing you're not is medicine hawkers. They don't handle *bandidos* the way you two do."

"That there is your opinion," said Raider, shrugging.

"You still don't appreciate the reality of your situation, do you?" Magrue was pacing back and forth before the bars of the cell as he talked—like an actor delivering lines on a stage. "Here you sit, in Sheriff Busby's jail, and we can fix it, easy, so you sit here damn near forever, or else get you ridden out of town on a rail. If worse comes to worst you might even get shot while trying to escape. Point is, we've got you by the balls, gentlemen, and the sooner you realize that, the sooner we can get around to seeing how we can let you go."

"What do you want, Magrue?" asked Raider. "Exactly."

"Answers. Clean, honest answers to a few simple questions. First—why are you two really here in Tesqua?"

Doc glanced at Raider. "Shall we tell him?"

Raider picked up the cue. "Okay, Doc. You do it. You're better at tellin' things than I am."

"You're right in figurin' the medicine wagon's

just an excuse, Magrue. It gets us into a place, lets us meet folks and get acquainted. It also throws folks off, so they don't get suspicious. Meanwhile, we get the lay of the land. There's always somethin' around just waitin' for somebody smart to take it. Might be jewels in somebody's house. Or a safe with cash in it—off it goes in the wagon so's we can take our time opening it, later. It's like hunting. We never know exactly what we're gonna get, just that *something*'ll turn up. But let me say right off, we haven't taken anything in this town of yours, yet. That's the honest truth, just like the rest of it."

Afer a moment of thought, Magrue nodded and said, "I see." He glanced at Busby. "Mind leaving us alone a few minutes, Harold?"

"Anything you say," said Busby. He rose heavily and left by the front door, taking his sack of pinyon nuts with him.

Magrue faced Doc and Raider again. "I am pleased to learn that you are honest crooks," he said. "Not that I condone thievery. But a man with his own self-interest in mind is, frankly, easier to deal with—more predictable. Now let me ask another question. You seem to know this Professor Ashley and his daughter pretty well. Why are *they* really here?"

"Like they say," said Doc. "Old Spanish pots and pans in some pueblo. Sounds crazy, but that's what professors do, I guess."

"If they're really professors, maybe." Magrue took Busby's chair, sat in it, and crossed his legs. "And it could be Ashley's what he says he is. For the time being, let's give him the benefit of the doubt. Even so, it wouldn't do for him to find these old Spanish artifacts he's after and then go back east with them."

"Why not?" ask Raider.

"Perhaps I'd better explain a few things, so we all know better just where we stand," said Magrue. He found cigars in his pocket, offered one to Raider, who accepted, and to Doc, who politely shook his head. In a moment, layers of pungent cigar smoke were filling the room.

"As you've probably learned by now," said Magrue, leaning back in leisurely fashion, "some people here in Tesqua resent everything I've done for the community. Before I came this town was rotting away and ready to die. It's the Spanish, as they call themselves, of course. Never did have any get-up-and-go. Look at the way they drop everything and go to sleep in the middle of the day. It was probably the siesta that destroyed the Spanish empire in Coronado's time. Anyway, I came here when I was assigned as Indian agent, saw how it was, and decided to do something about it. The first thing they needed here was officials with gumption, from the mayor on down. I picked the right men, from the Anglos mostly, got 'em elected or appointed. I opened up the markets for the cattle and sheep they raise, the leatherwork and weaving they do, and even put the little distillery here on its feet, making shipments to the outside now, bringing money in. A lot of 'em still don't appreciate it and it's easy to see why. If they'd rather sleep all day, they can't share all this new prosperity or take part in any of it."

"I take it you get *your* share, though," said Raider dryly.

"Of course," Magrue answered quickly. "Would you expect me to do all this—it amounts to running everything—for nothing?"

"No," said Raider. "That there I wouldn't expect."

"Now, since I am not a salaried official," Magrue continued blandly, "I must find other ways to be remunerated. Some of these ways might draw criticism from folks on the outside who don't know the way things are here in Tesqua. Who don't realize that without somebody to run the town right it would just die off, the same as a dozen other settlements in this territory. And that brings me back to this professor and his daughter."

"Huh?" asked Doc. "What have they got to do with it?"

"We're in a state of transition here," said Magrue, "while I get the town on its feet. Out of necessity, we cut a few corners, bend a few regulations. The last thing we need, right now, is attention from back east. If Ashley finds what he's looking for it'll make a big stir—not only professors but government officials flocking out here. They'll throw up their hands in pious horror and put the town right back where it was, with all my work gone for nothing."

"What you really mean," said Raider, "is they'll throw out you and all your hand-picked men and maybe send you to prison."

"There's that danger, too," said Magrue. "Folks never like to see a public benefactor properly rewarded for what he does."

"Okay, Magrue. We understand each other. Right on the mark, I'd say. But I still don't know how me and Doc fit into all this—or where all this talk is gettin' to."

"What we're getting to is this. Professor Ashley mustn't find these artifacts he's after. Or if he does, he mustn't take them back with him. And you two might be just the ones to see he doesn't succeed."

"Now, how in hell are we supposed to do *that?*" Raider asked.

Magrue blew a smoke ring and watched it rise to the ceiling. "Miss Ashley asked my help in providing an escort to ride out to Spanish Rock and the Zama Pueblo. I could have sent someone, or gone myself, for that matter, but that wouldn't do. If they found out later that their escort had something to do with their failure they could raise a stink that would be just as bad as drawing national attention. But if a couple of strangers like yourself got in the way, well, all they could do is complain."

Raider nodded. "I reckon I understand now. Just one thing. Why should Doc and I do something like this? What's in it for us?"

Magrue smiled. "You'll be paid. We'll discuss how much in a moment—it'll be worth your while, be assured of that. The most important persuasion, however, is not what you stand to gain but what you will avoid."

"How's that again?" Raider asked, crinkling his brows.

"Take a look at your surroundings, gentlemen. Not very choice. You'll be facing a long time if you decide not to cooperate. Might even drive you to suicide. That, or getting shot while trying to escape. All kinds of things might happen. Things to keep you from shooting off your mouths anyplace else. But we don't have to look at the dark side of it like this, do we, gentlemen?"

"Okay, Magrue," said Raider. "We see the carrot, and we see the stick. What's next?"

"Ways and means," said Magrue. "Details. And let's hope our little discussion now takes a more pleasant turn."

CHAPTER SEVEN

It was siesta time. Everybody in Tesqua, in the hot, early afternoon, with sun burning clear in the high, thin air, was sleeping. Well, nearly everybody. Raider wasn't sleeping. He was off someplace with Professor Ashley, helping him pick out the food supplies he'd need for the pack trip to Spanish Rock—which meant that the storekeeper wherever they were wasn't sleeping, though he was probably yawning and wishing he could get back to it.

And Doc certainly wasn't sleeping. Nor Genevieve, stretched out beside him. They were in bed, in Doc and Raider's hotel room, and they were jaybird naked.

Doc rolled to one side, leaned his head on his elbow, and glanced at Genevieve. Her blond hair was a molten golden spill on the pillow, and her breasts, flattened a little by their own weight, were spreading themselves out kind of like great domes of custard pudding. He liked the sight of her and he liked the aura that surrounded her—a smell of fertility, like when you get to the inside of a fermenting haystack.

She saw him gazing at her and she smiled and sighed. "I don't know which I like better," she said. "When we're making love or when we're resting like this."

"I do," said Doc, grinning. "The resting's just something that's gotta be done."

"It's true, isn't it," she said. "For everything you
80

want to do there are ten things you don't want to do."

"Seems that way sometimes," said Doc, barely listening, mostly just admiring her.

"Father's project, for example," she said. "All this preparation, all this journeying, just to find those artifacts. Anyway, I'm glad you and Mr. Raider decided to help us. I don't think we could have done it without you."

"Maybe not even with us. We're not there yet. Lot of things could still happen, maybe."

"I'm aware of the dangers," said Genevieve soberly. "And all the other obstacles. Not the least of which is the Indians themselves. I'm wondering now if they'll be cooperative."

Doc shrugged. "You never know about Injuns."

"Joe Sunbird's not so sure how they'll react."

"Who?"

"That funny little man Father picked up somewhere. He's half Indian, I think. Father's impressed with his knowledge of Indian ways, but I'm not so sure about him. It doesn't take much to sell Father a bill of goods."

Doc cocked his head curiously. "You didn't tell Raider and me somebody else was comin' along."

"I suppose we forgot. It's all been so hectic. Anyway, Father's engaged this man as a guide."

"Joe Sunbird, huh? Look, Jenny, maybe it'd be a good idea if I checked him out. He might be okay, but then he might not be."

"If you wish. He's easy enough to find. He hangs around the back door of the posada. He does little chores and the bartender passes him drinks. I *think* that's the arrangement."

"I'll find out soon enough. Meanwhile—" He ran his palm down the smooth contours of her torso until it reached the golden triangle of her pubic hair.

"No," she said, shaking her head. "Not that I don't want to. But Father and Mr. Raider'll be back any moment now."

"Goddamn!" said Doc, frowning, withdrawing his hand.

"My sentiments, exactly," said Genevieve, sighing even more deeply.

The rear courtyard of the inn was a tiny arena in the sun, surrounded by sunbaked 'dobe walls. Doc saw the sleeping man, his head and shoulders against a wall, a floppy straw sombrero covering his face, his legs in loose cotton trousers spread out before him.

Doc stood over him. "You Joe Sunbird?"

The man moved with agonizing slowness. First he raised his hand and tilted the brim of the straw hat so that he could look out from under it. He looked and blinked—one long, slow blink. His face, a nest of wrinkles, resembled the surface of a walnut. A black patch covered what had once been his left eye. After an extended pause, he spat to one side, looked at Doc again, and said, "You got a drink?"

"No," said Doc.

"Then get the fuck away," said Joe Sunbird.

"We're talkin'," said Doc. "About Professor Ashley, and how you're goin' with him."

"In a pig's ass," said Joe. "Go away. This here's siesta time—don't you know that?"

"It's drinkin' time," said Doc. "After we talk."

Joe Sunbird came erect, moving his shoulders from the wall. "You ain't shittin' me, are you, señor?"

"Get yourself up, if you can, and we'll go in the bar and talk."

The half-breed shook his head. "Not the bar. They don't let me in there. You gotta fetch me a drink."

"Okay. If I get the right answers."

"What the hell answers you talking about, *primo?*"

"I think you know, maybe. You know who I am, and a lot more you pretend you don't. Seth Magrue sent you to join up with Ashley, didn't he?"

"Magrue!" Joe Sunbird spat to one side again. "With that one, I think a *tigre* piss in his mother's milk."

Doc cocked his head. He could usually judge when a man was telling the truth or otherwise, and Joe's reaction, he believed, now answered one of his questions. It was a good bet Joe hadn't been sent by Magrue and was on his own. But there was still more Doc had to know. "Okay, Joe," he said. "Why *did* you offer your services to Ashley?"

"Huh? Why not?" The half-breed shrugged deeply. "Good way to get whiskey. He agrees to take some along."

"Part of your pay, is that it? Most of it, I'll bet. Well, that's your business. But what I'm interested in is what you're givin' in return. What the hell do you know about the country and the Indians, anyway?"

"Everything," said Joe firmly. "Been all my life here. Half Indian, half Spanish, but neither'll have much to do with me. Anglos won't, either, 'cause they don't like *anybody*. So fuck 'em all. Had to wander around; had to learn the country. Got myself into the pueblos now and then, learned all about *them*. What you want to know? Which girls from which tribe are the best piece of ass? The answer is the Zama, where we're goin'."

Doc frowned for a moment as he thought that over. Then he said, "Miss Ashley tells me you're not so sure the Zamas'll be so friendly when we get there."

Shrugging again with his bony shoulders, Joe Sunbird looked more than ever like a scarecrow. "They ain't got nothin against us in particular, but Magrue left a bad taste in their mouths. Cheatin' 'em blind, the way he does all the tribes."

"Heard rumors like that," said Doc, nodding. "Just how does he do it, anyway?"

"Government sends all kinds of stuff to the tribes. Flour, sugar, cloth, stuff to farm with—a hundred goddamn plows, last shipment. They send it because Magrue, as agent, reports the tribes are half starving and need it. Well, they ain't too well off, but they ain't half starvin', either. So Magrue gives 'em maybe twenty percent of the stuff and they sign for all of it. If they don't he'll report they're in good shape, and the government won't send nothin'. They go along with it 'cause twenty percent's better'n nothin'."

"How does Magrue dispose of the stuff?"

"Buyers come in, from here and there, and he delivers out in the desert somewhere, at night, mostly. He's careful—hardly anybody ever knows about it. Except me, 'cause I know every fuckin' thing."

"How come you don't snitch on Magrue to somebody?"

"Why the hell should I? Don't give a shit, long as I can get a few drinks and folks leave me alone. Besides, Magrue slips me some whiskey now and then. He ain't *all* sonofabitch, you know. Just a large part of him is."

"So I noticed," Doc said dryly. "Okay, Joe, those are pretty good answers. Better'n I expected. Raider and I will let you come along, I guess; maybe you will be of some help, at that."

"You gonna get me a drink now?"

"A whole bottle, Joe," said Doc, smiling. "Stay right where you are."

Later that afternoon, at the blacksmith's, where Raider was getting new shoes for two of the horses, Doc finally managed to pull his partner aside and tell him what he'd learned from Joe Sunbird.

Raider frowned. "You don't think he's lyin'?"

"No reason for him to."

"Well, it makes sense. That's about how Magrue would do it. All we gotta do now is get the goods on him."

"Evidence and all that," said Doc, nodding. "Pinkerton's bad enough on the legal ins and outs, and this time the client's the government, which makes it even worse. We could witness one of these here moonlight transfers of Magrue's and try to arrest him ourselves, but it wouldn't hold water. What we need is a U.S. marshal, or somebody like that. There oughta be one in Santa Fe."

"Maybe we oughta have him standin' by."

"I was thinkin' the same," said Doc. "Okay, who goes? You or me?"

"Toss you." Raider produced a coin.

"Heads it's me, tails it's you," said Doc.

Raider tossed. "Heads."

"Lemme see that."

"Don't you trust me?"

"Sure. About as far as I could throw a bull by his balls." Doc glanced at the coin on the back of Raider's hand, saw that it was indeed heads, and sighed and nodded.

"Wait till we're on the way to Spanish Rock," said Raider. "Then slip off and ride to Santa Fe. That way nobody'll notice and get suspicious. While you're there you might as well telegraph Denver and tell 'em what we learned. Then hightail it back and catch up with us at Spanish Rock."

Doc tilted his head to one side and regarded Raider with an expression of doubt. "Rade, goddamn it," he said, "you lay off Genevieve while I'm gone, you hear?"

Raider only grinned at him. Wolfishly. "Thought you didn't want to get tangled up permanent with her."

"What the hell's that got to do with it?"

"Then what do you care if you don't have her exclusive?"

"You just lay off her, that's all!" said Doc, hotly. "I'll personally castrate you, by God, if you don't!"

"Anytime you want to try," said Raider.

"Oh, shit," said Doc, "let's get these goddamn horses shoed and start things rollin'."

West of Tesqua and the gorge of the Brazos, the land began its sharper rise toward the Great Divide, the watershed of the continent, where all streams arose, then flowed east or west. They could see the distant blue ridge of it on the shimmering horizon. Although the going didn't seem to be uphill, the horses were plodding a little slower than usual, sweating a little harder, puffing a little earlier. They rode in single file, Joe Sunbird, astride a scrawny yellow horse he'd procured somewhere; on the point a hundred yards or so ahead, Raider, Doc, Genevieve, and Professor Ashley grouped together, the packhorses strung out behind them.

There was even less vegetation here than on

the stretch between Santa Fe and Tesqua. The dry earth, scarred with arroyos, was dotted with scrubby, blue-green growth, and most of the level areas were pocked with prairie-dog holes. The tiny rodents sat on their haunches and watched the intruders pass.

Raider pointed his finger at one, as though he held a gun. "Know what they can do? Duck bullets. Yup. They can see 'em comin'."

"I don't believe it!" said Genevieve, half laughing.

"God's honest truth," said Raider. "I've drawn a bead and shot at lots of 'em. Never got one yet. And when I aim, I don't miss."

"Do you mean to say you'd shoot one of those harmless little creatures?"

"If I was hungry, I damn sure would. And the times I shot at 'em, I was."

Genevieve shuddered a little. "Even so—"

"Rade don't let much stand in his way when he wants something," said Doc smugly. Raider glanced at him and he grinned. Raider knew damned well what he was up to—making Raider unattractive to Genevieve—and Doc knew damned well he knew it.

Professor Ashley was barely following this exchange; he was gazing ahead absentmindedly. He didn't seem to be overwarm, even in the glaring sun, in his long linen duster and tweed cap with the fore-and-aft bills, and Doc supposed he was already putting together in his mind the long history-piece he'd write when and if he uncovered those precious artifacts he was after.

They had left Tesqua in the early morning, and now the sun was reaching its zenith in the blue, unblemished sky. Raider called a noon halt, and they dismounted, then doled out a few precious

drops from the water casks for the horses. Genevieve made coffee and sandwiches of soft tortillas
and smoked chicken meat they'd procured in the
settlement. Doc and Raider drifted off to one side,
so they could talk.

" 'Bout time for you to ride off," Raider said to
Doc.

"I'm goin'; don't push me," said Doc. "Before
I go, though, I want to make sure you got everything figured out right."

"Like what?"

"Well, Magrue expects us to keep the professor
from bringin' back those pots and pans if he finds
them. How're we gonna make that look good and
still keep Magrue from gettin' suspicious of us?"

"Ain't decided exactly, yet," said Raider.
"There'll be some way. We just got to play the
cards the way they fall. We might even have to
take Genevieve and the professor into our confidence, so they can tell some cock-and-bull story
about not finding the damn things, even if they do.
Anyway, the important thing is to keep Magrue
thinkin' we're as crooked as he is. That way, it'll
be easier to catch him red-handed when he sells off
some of that government stuff next time."

"Well," said Doc, frowning with a touch of
doubt, "let's hope it works out like we think it will."

"It better work out *some* way," said Raider, nodding. "Neither one of the two Pinkerton brothers is
too happy with us these days. We usually deliver
the goods, sure—but we always do it our own way,
and maybe bust a regulation or two while we're at
it. I get the feelin' they'd like to be rid of us—
find some excuse to let us go."

"Then let them, damn it," said Doc. "They don't
pay all that good in the first place."

"They don't," Raider agreed. "But we sure get

to see the country. If we didn't have this job we might have to settle down someplace. Can you imagine you and me workin' at some job somewhere and comin' home at night to a bunch o' kids sprawlin' underfoot?"

"Can't bear the thought," groaned Doc. "It's why I didn't quit long ago."

"Well, there you are. So tend to business, Doc. Get your ass to Santa Fe."

Doc looked hard at his partner. "I keep havin' the feeling you're setting me up, Rade."

"Why would I do that?"

"For a chance to roll in the grass with Genevieve. You'd set up your own mother for that."

"Maybe I would," said Raider, grinning. "But you still better get goin'."

"Okay, I will. Just don't get too sure of yourself, Rade. I might make it back sooner'n you think."

"You know where to find me," said Raider, holding his grin. "Anytime."

CHAPTER EIGHT

It was some kind of natural law, Doc figured; unexpected delays came along in bunches whenever you were really in a hurry. According to how much hurry you were in, too. His hurry was mighty big this time. The more time Raider had to work on Genevieve during his absence, the more likely Raider was to succeed—hell, Doc owed it to Genevieve to get back as fast as he could.

But something was trying to keep him from that. Indian spirits, for all he knew. First, he turned into a canyon he thought would be a shortcut and fetched up against a rock wall five miles farther on, which made it necessary to retrace his steps. When he came out of the canyon again, a thunderstorm passed over, darkening the sky and causing him to lose his bearings On top of that, the rain came down in such buckets he had to find shelter under a rocky overhang and sit it out for an hour or so. That wasn't all. The storm sent a flash flood roaring down an arroyo, which he couldn't cross, so he had to wait a few more hours for the waters to subside.

It was nighttime by then. He would have kept going, using the stars to find his way, but the claybank mare Raider had lent him just wasn't a night horse and kept picking its way cautiously no matter how hard he tried to urge it on. He gave up, halted for the night, and tried to get some sleep. A cougar came sniffing around, spooked the horse, and Doc had to chase it. Way to hell and gone. By the time he found it again it was dawn.

He thought he was on his way at last by midday, and not too far from Santa Fe, and that was when the horse almost stepped on a fat, tawny rattler, which buzzed its tail, startling hell out of the horse and, as a matter of fact, out of Doc, too. If Doc hadn't been so startled he would have held on better when the horse reared and started to buck. He sailed through the air and hit the ground hard, on his rump. The claybank mare, galloping wildly, disappeared over a ridge.

"To hell with you, then, you dumb critter!" Doc called after it.

He walked the rest of the way to Santa Fe.

The town was growing, as all towns in the Southwest were, but it didn't have the clapboard and ramshackle look of the new cow and mining towns farther north, up Kansas and Colorado way. It had been here a long time as capital of the territory. The center of things was around the old governor's palace, a low, sprawling adobe building with *portale*s over the walkways and a dusty plaza in front of it. Coal-oil street lamps, recently built, gave light to this part of town.

Doc tried the courthouse, where a U.S. marshal might be, and found everything locked. Same with the telegraph office at the railroad station. His duty done for the time being, he said to himself to hell with it and headed for the inn.

The desk clerk was a small, fussy man of Spanish extraction—some kind of queer, Doc would bet —who managed to make his nose look as though he were fastidiously pulling it away from the grimy, sweaty traveler who stood before him. When Doc pulled out a roll of bills to pay for the room, he became more attentive. Two hours later, Doc came down, bathed and shaved, his clothes smoothed out as best he could. He headed for the dining room and ordered a steak.

As in all towns of Spanish flavor, folks ate late here, taking their revels afterward, until the small hours of the morning, and catching up with their sleep the next day at siesta time. The room was crowded, buzzing with conversation and laughter. Most of the diners looked well dressed and prosperous; none paid much attention to Doc at his corner table, and that was all right with Doc.

When the waitress came back with Doc's steak, she said, "Will that be all, sir?"

Doc took a closer look at her this time. Pretty little thing, kind of round-faced, and well curved. Not fat, just pigeon plump. She was smiling at him, and her eyes were smiling, too. Sometimes waitresses and such smiled at you with their lips, but their eyes didn't join in.

"Maybe some dessert later," said Doc. "What's your name, señorita?"

"Conchita."

"That's a pretty name. Short for Concepción, right?"

"Well, it is not much shorter."

They both laughed at that.

"My name's Doc. Doc Weatherbee."

"Pleased to meet you, señor. You are a stranger here, *verdad?*"

"Guess that's easy enough to see," said Doc. He nodded toward a crowded table at the far end of the room where the talk and laughter was particularly animated and the guests were raising toasts with red wine, one after the other. "What's the big party over there?"

"Oh, that is the governor's table, señor. It is his birthday. He is the small, thin man at the head of the table; the one who is so quiet."

"So that there's Governor Wallace, huh? Heard tell of him. General in the Civil War. Yup. General Lew Wallace."

"He was a soldier? I did not know."

"Grant you he don't look like one. Sometimes soldiers don't."

"I was thinking also that he is—how do you say it? —*un autor de historias.*"

Doc nodded. "Heard tell of that, too. Wrote *The Fair God*, about the Spanish conquest of Mexico. Ain't read it yet, and probably never will. Don't have much time for readin'."

"He is working now on a wonderful story. About Rome and the Holy Land in the time of the Savior. It is to be called *Ben Hur*, I think."

"That so? How come you know all about what the governor's working on?"

"I have, uh, certain gentleman friends in the palace." There was something off-center about her smile this time; it was the smile of someone saying something in a roundabout way.

"I'd expect someone as pretty as you would have a whole passel of gentleman friends," said Doc. He cocked his head to one side as he grinned. "Wouldn't mind bein' one of 'em."

At this, Conchita glanced quickly from side to side as though to be sure no one was listening. "It is possible, señor. But it requires, well, *un poco dinero.*"

"Money?" Doc's eyebrows rose in mild surprise.

"A waitress does not earn much pay. I must do what I can, do you understand?"

"Sure. It just surprises me a little. If you're puttin' out for pay, how come you're not in the bar with the other gals?"

Conchita shrugged. "It is better this way. No trouble with the police, and I can pick and choose."

Doc stared back at her for a moment, then laughed. "Well, Conchita," he said finally, "you got yourself a customer. How do we get together?"

"It will take two hours for me to get away. You have a room here?"

"Two-sixteen."

"All night, señor?"

"You said it."

"Ten dollars."

"You *do* come high," said Doc. He continued to inspect her. "Well, I reckon you'll be worth it."

"Half now," said Conchita. "Put it under the plate."

Doc produced a five-dollar bill, slipped it under the plate surreptitiously, and held his grin as Conchita smiled, nodded, and moved off. He watched her tight little buttocks clicking back and forth as she walked away. Yup. Bound to be worth it. He was stiffening a bit already in his trousers and had all but lost interest in the steak in front of him.

In his room, Doc kept looking impatiently at his nickel-plated pocket watch that had miraculously survived his ignominious fall from the claybank mare. It wasn't quite two hours yet, but he'd had a couple of drinks after dinner in the bar to warm his innards and had become bored with the noisy crowd there, to say nothing of the way his groin was beginning to tingle in anticipation.

There was a small desk in the room, an inkpot with a pen beside it, and a sheaf of letter paper. Doc sat there and, to kill the time, began to compose the telegraph message he'd send first thing in the morning. (And, he reminded himself, he'd better remember to drag himself out of bed for it, too.)

The trick in writing these messages was to cut

down on words to make them as short as possible. The Pinkerton brothers, true to their Scottish ancestry, kept a close eye on pennies that could be saved—sometimes so close they failed to see what else was going on. He wrote:

Have uncovered modus operandi. *Need few more weeks to witness execution of same. Please wire additional funds for expense account. Cannot do this on peanuts. Your obedient servant, Weatherbee.*

He frowned for a moment at what he had written, then carefully crossed out the part about the peanuts.

There was a knock on the door. Doc rose immediately, went to it, opened it, and saw Conchita standing there. She had changed into a billowing skirt and a blouse that wanted to fall off one bare shoulder; she had one hand on her hip and her head tilted to one side in a classic, saucy pose.

"Come on in," said Doc, grinning, "and make yourself at home."

She did just that. Faster than Doc expected. He himself, once aroused, liked to get to the business at hand without a lot of nonsensical delay—the way some women, for example, kept pretending they weren't going to do anything right up to the moment in which they finally did it—but Conchita was even more direct than he would have been. The moment she closed the door behind her she started on his shirt buttons, and, as he picked up the chore, she stepped back and wriggled out of her own loose blouse. Alternately then, she tore at his clothes and then her own, until both faced each other in only their skin, and after that, still vibrating with energy, she grabbed his up-slanted cock and pulled him by it to the bed, pushing him down there, leaping upon him, bouncing and squirming all over him.

"You like?" she said, with a teasing smile.

"Hell, yes!" said Doc.

"You take it easy, *querido*," she said. "I will do everything."

Everything it was, Doc learned presently. Everything he'd ever heard of—and maybe a few things he hadn't. Conchita, tireless, was never still. She started atop him, lowering herself in a sitting position as he penetrated, and when, by working herself up and down that way vigorously, she brought him almost to his climax, she pulled off suddenly, turned herself around, and bestrode him facing the other way. After a few moments of that position, she changed to another, then another and another, receiving him in various crevices of her gyrating body, sometimes partly, sometimes all the way, taking his cock between her breasts, in the crack of her buttocks, into her tightened thighs, and in her hot, sucking mouth, her tongue flickering on it like the tip of a bullwhip, her hands busy fingertipping and grabbing him all over, her staccato movements without pause, so that he had not a moment's rest. But in spite of this, she kept him from exhausting himself too soon, skillfully turning to the next variation just when he felt himself about to end the round.

Doc couldn't hold out forever—though, by golly, he thought, he was doing his best to—and Conchita finally satisfied him the first time, grinning at him in delight and what was probably pride in her own prowess as he squinched his eyes and groaned with pleasure.

And she didn't let him rest even then. Moments later she was squirming all over him again, arousing him for a second go-round. Doc wondered how

many she'd manage to get out of him before the
evening was over. "Sugar," he said, sighing, "the
way you go at it, I just might break my own record
this time."

Doc never did find out about breaking his record
because somewhere along the line he lost count.
And that was why he wasn't sure how long he and
Conchita had been enjoying themselves when the
interruption came.

The room door slammed open. Men came in. In
the first, startled moment, Doc wasn't sure how
many. The room was dim, and he couldn't tell.
Too many, too damned many, that was for sure.
Anything above zero at a time like this was too
many. Besides, instead of waiting to count, he was
already springing from the bed, knocking Conchita
to the floor more roughly than he would have preferred to, and leaping toward the dim figures that
were halfway across the room by now.

There was a squat, stocky figure in front of him.
Something familiar about it. But Doc wasn't pausing to find out whether he and this person had been
previously introduced. He lashed out with a hard
right hook, and his fist met what felt like a huge
bale of hay, much too dense to knock over. No
more than three seconds had passed since Doc
had sprung from the bed, but that was time enough
for him to berate himself inwardly for hanging his
gunbelt off to the side, where it wasn't handy.
Conchita just hadn't given him a chance to set
things up with his usual caution.

Since the first blow failed to knock his antago-
nist down, or, for that matter, move him backward
any, Doc immediately considered a second, and
even tensed himself up for it. He never got it off.
There was a sound in his skull like a two-bladed
ax thunking into a huge tree, only ten times as

loud as that; there was a meteor display in front of his eyes, and after that, blackness.

Once, back east, when Doc had had his portrait made, the photographer had let him look at the ground glass in the back of the camera, and had twisted the lens as he looked until the upside-down image came into focus. It was like that now. The face above him was milky and fuzzy in outline at first, then became sharper after he had blinked at it several times. He was aware, as he stared, of the throbbing pain in his head. He'd been hit hard and fast—pistol butt, for a guess. The coal-oil lamps had been turned up and the room was brighter. The froglike, upside-down face glaring down at him belonged to Cristóbal, the *bandido* Doc and Raider had stopped before he could ravish Genevieve on the way to Tesqua.

"Hey, señor!" said Cristóbal, grinning. "You out cold. Good thing I didn't kill you!"

"Yeah, that's a good thing," said Doc, trying not to grimace from the throbbing in his head. "So we agree. Okay, what's next? What in hell do you want?"

"You," said Cristóbal, nodding at him.

Doc, still shaky, scrambled to his feet. The men in the room, gathered in a rough half-circle around him, allowed him to do so. Doc noticed Cristóbal's thin and hollow-eyed companion, Transito, and two of the other *bandido*s who had accosted Genevieve and the professor, "Me, huh?" said Doc, dusting himself off, not so much because he needed dusting as to give his hands something to do, and to distract the four men a little while he tried to think things over.

"*Si*," said Cristóbal cheerfully. "We follow you and the others out of sight, then we see your tracks go off. We follow them, too, and pretty soon find out you here in Santa Fe."

"Okay, I'm in Santa Fe," said Doc. "What the hell's that got to do with anything?"

"I don't know," said Cristóbal, shrugging. "But Señor Magrue, he say if you go anyplace but Spanish Rock he want to see you, *pronto.*"

"He does, huh? Suppose I don't want to see him."

Cristóbal laughed. "Hey, señor, you think we go back without you? We bring you to Señor Magrue if we have to carry you." He nodded at Transito, who was stepping forward, holding his pistol by the barrel and brandishing it. "You want to go sleep again, señor? That how you want it?"

"Okay, you got the cards," said Doc. "What do we do—leave right away?"

"Momentito," said Cristóbal, his wide mouth spreading in an even broader grin. He glanced at Conchita, who was huddled, wide-eyed, in a corner, holding her crumpled blouse and skirt in front of her so that she had at least some cover. "First, we take this señorita and finish up for you, no?"

"Touch me and I'll scream!" said Conchita in Spanish.

"Scream and I'll kill you," said Cristóbal calmly in the same language.

The other three held Doc—a pistol to his head —and made him watch while Cristóbal enjoyed himself with Conchita. Then each in turn traded places with one of those holding Doc and banged away at the girl. She made her face cold and herself rigid and endured the quadruple rape without so much as a murmur. Doc admired her courage, and it was nice to be admiring something, but it didn't help matters one damn bit.

It was a show Doc would have preferred not to

watch. He'd never been much for shows of this kind—participating was a hell of a lot better—but with a pistol at his temple all through the demonstration, he was forced to witness everything. If there was anything good to this whole bucket of crawdads, it was that Conchita kept herself a stone statue and didn't put out for them the way she had for Doc. They would never know what they had missed.

At last they were finished. Muttering directions, they herded Doc out of the room. As he entered the hallway, it occurred to him that Conchita would rush downstairs as soon as they were gone and report what had happened; in that case, somebody might follow after them and give Doc a chance to escape.

The same idea must have occurred suddenly to Cristóbal. He came to an abrupt halt. He angled his head back at the room and murmured to Transito, *"La muchacha."* Then he ran his finger across his throat.

"Si," said Transito, grinning to show his bad teeth.

He whirled and headed back for the room door. Doc saw him draw a hunting knife from the sheath on his belt as he opened the door and entered.

CHAPTER NINE

In the clear air, Spanish Rock was visible long before they came to it; it remained visible for what seemed endless hours as they continued toward it, never seeming to be any nearer, as though it were withdrawing from them as fast as they approached. It was a great column rising from the scree of the desert floor, flat-topped like the other, lower mesas in the region, but towering, imposing, dominating, the throne of some savage god whose domain was all that could be seen from its summit.

The horses were straining, and Joe Sunbird advised holding them back. "They smell water," he said to Raider. "They want to run to it, lather themselves up, and drop dead before they get to it. Stupid sonsabitches. I tell you something, señores. Water, it will kill you every time."

He tilted his pint bottle of Millikan's Squirrel Whiskey and swigged from it, stuck it back in the saddle bag, then adjusted his black eyepatch, which he'd dislodged slightly in the process.

"Not as quick as that stuff'll kill *you,* Joe," said Raider, grinning.

"Shit!" said Joe. "I run on the stuff, like a cougar runs on meat and a bird runs on horse turds. Everybody runs on something different. Didn't you know that, señor?"

Raider laughed. "Maybe you do, at that. I've seen some strange hombres in my time, and I reckon you're one of 'em."

"Goddamn right," said Joe Sunbird, nodding with self-satisfaction.

Professor Ashley had laid in a supply of Millikan's Squirrel, and each morning and evening, according to their agreement, he gave Joe his pint bottle. He nipped at the bottle at intervals and never seemed to get drunk. He rode straight and didn't stagger when he was dismounted and walking with his toed-in walk, which must have come from the Indian side of him. The only sign Raider could raise to tell that the whiskey was affecting him was in a curious opaqueness that came over his one good eye, as though to further block out the sight of the world, for which he hadn't much use.

Raider nodded toward the pillar of rock, where it shimmered in the distant heat waves rising from the desert floor. "Still a ways off," he said. "Be nightfall by the time we get there. We might surprise 'em too much, comin' in out of the dark."

"We ain't surprising nobody," said Joe, spitting to one side. "They see us."

"This far?"

"Believe me, señor, they see us. They have the eyes of eagles. The eagle is their *espiritu principal*."

Genevieve, riding on the other side of Joe, looked at him. "You mean like one of their gods—is that it?"

"Something like that," Joe said, shrugging. "It is hard to explain."

"I talked to some of the priests in Tesqua," said Genevieve. "It was my understanding all the Indians in the pueblos around here had become Christians."

"*Si*. They have. But that don't mean they give up their old ways. They have their gods, and also the white man's god. They figure that's pretty good, no? Whatever god they happen to need."

"What they're doin'," Raider said, grinning again, "is coverin' their bets."

Genevieve sighed. "Raider, that's close to blasphemy."

"Can't help that," said Raider. "It's what I think."

"And you always say what you think, I suppose," she said.

"Sometimes. Sometimes I just don't say nothin' at all."

She regarded him with interest. He'd caught her doing that several times in the past day or two. "You're a hard man to know, Raider. To really know, I mean."

"Not as hard as you think," said Raider, with a significant look.

She looked away without answering, but Raider knew very well she understood what he was really saying. A little time alone with him in the moonlight and they'd both get to know each other. Real good. He hadn't pushed it, however—not out of any respect for Doc and whatever claims he'd staked with Genevieve, but because his instinct told him she wouldn't be pushed; his best chance with her, if there was any chance at all, lay in a roundabout approach, the way you stalk any spooky game.

They continued their slow approach in silence. Professor Ashley, still in his linen duster in spite of the heat, lagged a little behind, gazing this way and that, living in a private world in his own head, answering pleasantly enough whenever spoken to, but essentially acting as though he were a million miles away from all of them.

In mid-afternoon, Joe, his eye on the horses, called a halt so that they could be watered slightly, and Raider agreed with him. Everybody hunkered down for a short rest, and this gave Raider a chance to talk to Ashley and his daughter alone.

Raider lit one of his butted cigars and puffed it absentmindedly, without inhaling. "Been meanin' to bring something up, Professor," he said. "Might not get another chance once we reach the rock, so I might as well say it now."

"Uh, yes. Quite," said Professor Ashley, obviously not knowing what Raider was getting to, and just as obviously not caring a great deal.

"If you find these here ancient pots and pans of yours," said Raider, "I want you to tuck 'em away good when we get back to Tesqua. And I want you to tell everybody there you didn't find a damn thing."

"Eh? How extraordinary!" said Ashley, staring.

"Why on earth should we do that?" asked Genevieve.

"Let me lay a coupla things on the table for you," continued Raider. "Maybe you heard, and maybe you didn't, but Magrue's stealin' the Indians blind, and everybody else along with 'em. You must've noticed he didn't want to help you get out to the Zama Pueblo. That's because he don't want you to find anything and stir up a big fuss that'll bring folks here, where they'll find out soon enough what he's up to. So it's best if you just tell him nothin' happened, clear out as fast as you can, and *then* announce what you've got, if there is anything."

"I still don't understand why we should do that," said Genevieve. "If Magrue doesn't want us to take back this archaeological treasure, well, that's his problem, not ours."

"It'll be your problem," Raider said solemnly. "Believe me, Magrue'll see to that. Let me tell it to you right out, the way it is. He'll have you killed."

"Killed?" Genevieve drew away in astonishment.

"This ain't the civilized East, Jenny," said Raider. "The sooner both o' you get that into your heads, the safer you'll be."

She grabbed a moment of thought out of the air. "Does this have something to do with the way Doc rode off so suddenly?"

Raider nodded. "Don't want to explain exactly, but, yes, that's part of it."

"You're not all you appear to be," she said, inspecting him closely. "Neither you nor Doc."

"If you want to think that way, go ahead," said Raider, shrugging. "But if you want to stay alive, better do like I say. Okay?"

"All right, Raider," she said. "We'll play it your way. Do you agree, Father?"

"What? Oh, yes. Certainly. Whatever you say, Genevieve." He was already staring again at the distant horizon.

It was still light when at last they reached the foot of Spanish Rock. The great mesa loomed more than three hundred feet above them, silhouetted against a sky that had turned scarlet in the west, as the sun lowered itself behind this curtain like some fiery, malevolent eye. Joe Sunbird muttered superstitious things about red skies being ill omens, but Raider didn't listen closely.

Raider was watching the small procession that was coming toward them from the mesa, obviously to meet them. They had halted now and, still mounted, were four abreast, Genevieve and the professor raising themselves slightly in their saddles and looking toward the approaching delegation curiously, Raider and Joe relaxed in the way of men ready to respond swiftly to any trouble.

There were five Indians approaching them, and in a moment it became clear that one was a young woman. The men wore slip-over shirts and cotton trousers; she was dressed in a velvet blouse and a voluminous Spanish skirt. All were adorned with silver and turquoise jewelry.

As the four men halted a few yards from the newcomers, the young woman stepped forward. *Pretty little thing,* thought Raider; *Indian pretty, not imitation-white-woman pretty.* Her skin was the hue of finest tanned calf leather, and her eyes, slanted like Oriental eyes, were large, dark, and luminous. Her glossy black hair, secured by a headband, fell down to well below her shoulders.

"How," said Raider, raising his palm. "We come see you, make pow-wow."

With a faint, flickering smile, and with her eyes firm upon Raider, the girl said, "I assure you, sir, it's not necessary to talk to me that way. Ordinary English will do."

Raider's jaw fell in surprise. He hadn't expected good English. Good? A damn sight better than his own, the way this gal slung it, he had to admit. He recovered himself quickly and said, "Sorry. Didn't know. You must have had some schoolin'. Hell of a lot, at that."

The Indian girl smiled, which was the same as saying he'd guessed correctly, and then she said, "My name is Kara. I will be the interpreter, as you see." She turned and nodded at one of the men behind her. He was stocky and white-haired, peering at everyone with what seemed a touch of cautious amusement from alert little eyes deep in nests of woven wrinkles. "Tabaydeh is the *cacique.* I give you his greeting."

"Well, tell him we say howdy, too," said Raider. "And all best wishes. And any other way you can make it fancy."

"That won't be necessary," she said. "He sees what you say in your eyes."

"Handy trick," said Raider dryly. He relaxed a little more in the saddle. "Well, I reckon I'd better start with who we are, then I'll get around to explainin' why we're here. Main thing is, we mean no harm to anybody and, in fact, are kind of hopin' everything's gonna be real friendly. You want to tell the chief that much?"

As she relayed these words to Tabaydeh, Raider glanced at Joe Sunbird. He looked puzzled. He saw Raider looking at him and said, almost in a whisper, "They're usin' their own special language. It's almost like Tanoan or Kiowa, which they all speak, but different enough so's I can't follow it."

The girl faced Raider again and said, "Tabaydeh is ready to hear your story."

Raider began by introducing each member of the party in turn, himself included. When he mentioned Joe Sunbird's name, the girl nodded quickly, and he understood that they all knew Joe. "Now, Mr. Ashley here," said Raider, "is a famous history professor, and he wants to do some studyin' in your pueblo. Myself, I'm just kinda ridin' shotgun for the Ashleys."

There was another brief exchange in the Indian tongue, and then Kara said, "Tabaydeh would like to know what kind of history and how the professor proposes to study it."

"That there's too long a story to sit here and tell," said Raider. "Be easier all around if we go somewhere comfortable. One more thing I forgot. The professor brought some presents. He'd like to pass 'em out while we're all sittin' down."

Kara's smile broadened. "I would guess, Mr. Raider, that you're fishing for an invitation to dinner."

"To tell you the truth," Raider said, "that there is exactly what I had in mind."

As she spoke to the Indians this time, there was laughter. She turned to the visitors once more. "Welcome to Zama, which means, as nearly as I can translate it, 'Place of Beauty in the Sky.' Brace yourselves. It's a long climb to the top."

Everyone was silent as all, in single file, mounted the countless steps cut into the side of the rock, winding upward to the plateau atop the mesa.

At the top was a complete village of typical adobe houses clustered in random fashion around a central plaza that contained the pillbox structure of the kiva, or Indian place of worship. Professor Ashley, gazing about, seemed enchanted with it all; Raider, who had seen pueblos before, took it in stride. The houses had no entrance at the ground level but were all reached by ladders that led to the roofs, where trapdoors led to the interior. On many of the roofs there were rain cisterns, and vaselike *tinajas,* or water jugs, in which water from the valley below was stored, stood there against the walls. The men and women of the Zama tribe, Raider reflected, did a lot of climbing —he himself was puffing slightly from the long ascent—and their strong, wiry builds reflected this.

It was dark now, and the visitors were brought into a large central house, where they were invited to squat on blankets in the company of Tabaydeh, the chief, and several men who appeared to be his council of advisors. Torches lighted the interior and ventilation slots in the walls and ceiling had been somehow arranged to create a draft that drew off most of the smoke.

In a far corner a very old man, squatting silently, began to beat slowly on a drum that was a single skin stetched upon a circled frame with a handle.

A black, shallow bowl of fired clay appeared and was passed around. In it were little buttons that seemed to be the seeds and pods of some kind of plant. Raider, knowing what was happening, took one and passed the dish to Genevieve.

"What is it, an appetizer?" she asked.

Raider smiled slightly. "You could say that, maybe. Peyote. Kind of a cactus. The plains tribes pass around a stone pipe. Here, it's peyote—part of their religion, in a way."

Genevieve, following what the others were doing, placed one of the buttons in her mouth and began to chew on it.

Old Tabaydeh closed his eyes and began to sway back and forth, humming a chant that was almost inaudible.

Kara was beside Raider, watching him with what seemed to be slight amusement. He noticed her look, smiled back, and said, "Yup. Done this before."

"Did you see the colors?"

"Seen all kinds of things. In some ways, better'n whiskey, though I don't expect Joe Sunbird'll agree with that."

"It's different with different people," Kara said. "And a lot depends on the state of mind when one ingests it."

He gave her another momentary stare—one of many he'd been turning her way since meeting her. "I really didn't figure on finding someone like you here. That schooling you had. Must've been quite a bit. How come, anyway?"

Kara shrugged, and this in itself showed how she had taken on the white man's ways, for the shrug is not an Indian gesture. "Long ago, when I was small, Tabaydeh, who is very wise, decided we needed a really skillful interpreter here—one who knew not only the language but all the white man's customs. He made arrangements with a priest and sent me back east. It was after he'd tested many young girls; I seemed to have an ear for language. I suppose I could add many details to the story, but that, basically, is what happened."

"You like it better here, or back where you were?"

Avoiding his eyes, Kara stared at one of the flickering torches. After a moment's thought, she said, "It is not a question of what I like. I am here. It is my life. That is all."

"You mean you couldn't get out if you wanted?"

"We have no time to discuss this now, Mr. Raider," she said quickly. "Tabaydeh has many questions he wishes all of you to answer."

With Kara interpreting, the old chief began to put his questions to the visitors. Professor Ashley emerged from his cocoon of absentminded thought and supplied most of the answers. He told of his interest in Coronado's march to this region over three centuries before, of his researches, and of the clues that led him to believe the conquistadores had left a trove of artifacts in one of the pueblos. He mentioned the notation in Don Luis's family records that seemed to point to the Zama Pueblo. During his discourse, the presents were un-wrapped—jackknives, a pocket watch, saint's me-dallions, and, wonder of wonders to the Indians, a stereopticon with photo cards containing views of bucolic New England scenes and some of the great buildings and monuments in Washington, D.C. Tabaydeh and the others couldn't get over how real and three-dimensional the double photos looked when viewed through the lenses of the device.

Professor Ashley's eyes seemed to be gleaming now. An almost silly smile was on his thin, aristocratic lips. Raider made his own smile. The peyote was getting to him. That was the remarkable thing about peyote. You didn't even know when you were squirreled with it.

"So, you see," said Ashley, "we had one heck of a time getting here, if I may employ such slang to express my meaning. There was even a person, one Magrue, in Tesqua, who seemed to be standing in our way—at least he deigned to be very helpful."

Hearing this interpreted, the chief smiled and delivered a short speech, which Kara relayed to the professor. "It is a good thing that Señor Magrue was not helpful to you. For he is helpful only to those who are like him and anyone who is like Señor Magrue is an evil person. We thought, at first, Magrue might have sent you here. In that case, we would have sent you off again, perhaps by force. But now we see you are not of Magrue's kind and therefore you are welcome."

Raider slipped in a question for Kara. "How's he so damned sure the professor ain't in cahoots with that sidewinder, Magrue?"

"The peyote," she said, smiling. "One does not lie when one has eaten the sacred button."

"Didn't know it worked that way. But if you say so, I guess it does. Anyway, so much the better for the professor. So what about these old Spanish things he's after? Are they here, like he thinks?"

"That is a question," she said, "that only Tabaydeh can answer. And I do not think he will answer quickly. In the meantime, you must be our guests, and not bring up the subject, or you will offend

Tabaydeh. If he wishes to discuss it he will say so. When he is ready."

"When might that be?"

"Who knows? Tonight, tomorrow, a week, a year from now. Tabaydeh does not measure time as the white man does."

"Maybe he's got somethin' there," said Raider, grinning. He felt the peyote taking hold of him now. His head was getting light—floating off all by itself somewhere. Splotches of strange, rainbow-like colors were forming when he looked at the walls. It wasn't like being whiskey-drunk, however; he had the possession of all his faculties. On the other hand, there was at least one similarity. He was starting to feel horny.

He glanced at Genevieve. A silly smile, like the professor's, was on her face. It was his guess she was getting horny, too.

CHAPTER TEN

Doc Weatherbee was the only prisoner in the Tesqua County Jail. Seth Magrue and Sheriff Busby had seen to that—getting rid of a couple of drunks and disturbers of the peace who were delighted to be booted out into the street and told not to come back.

It was night and the curtains in the sheriff's office had been tightly drawn. Doc was spread-eagled against the wall of the cell, his wrists bound and trussed to the bars of the high, small window. His shirt had been removed; the gritty adobe wall pressed roughly against his face and chest.

Magrue, in his full wild West show regalia, stood at the open door of the cell, with the immensely fat Busby beside him, nervously popping handfuls of pinyon nuts into his mouth. Toadlike Cristóbal was in the cell, a coiled bullwhip in his hand.

"Well, Doc," said Magrue, almost pleasantly, but also quite firmly. "I tried to make this a nice, easy conversation, and I wasted more time on that than I usually do. Evidently you want to do this the hard way."

"Goddamn it, Magrue," said Doc—his tone of voice hitting a balance between how much he wanted to defy Magrue and how much he was genuinely alarmed now over what Magrue obviously had in mind—"nobody wants to do things the hard way. I told you everything I know. What do you want me to do? Make up stuff that ain't so?"

"Stubborn, aren't you? All the more reason for me to think you and your partner are something

113

more than ordinary medicine men. And you insult my intelligence when you expect me to believe that cock-and-bull story you tried to give me."

"Well, the truth ain't always nice and neat and wrapped up in a package with pretty ribbons. You been around enough to know that."

"The truth doesn't have a lot of holes in it, either," said Magrue. "You say you had a run-in with your partner over the girl, so you high-tailed it to Santa Fe just to get yourself a piece of ass. Lot of trouble to go to, just for a quick one."

"That kinda thing's worth a lotta trouble to some of us."

"It still doesn't explain what you wrote on that piece of paper." Magrue fished in his pocket for the paper Cristóbal had found on the hotel-room desk, uncrumpled it, and read it again. "Have uncovered *modus operandi*. Need few more weeks to witness execution of same. Please wire additional funds for expense account." He looked up. "That sounds like legal talk— policeman's talk—to me. Like you were drafting a telegram to somebody."

"Sure!" said Doc earnestly. "There's this madam I know back east, just like I told you. Real friendly with her, on account of I've always been a good customer. So, traveling all around the country like I do, I promised her I'd keep my eye open for new ways to do it, so's she could pass 'em on to her girls. That's what I meant by *modus operandi*—"

"And this is where it turns into a cock-and-bull story," interrupted Magrue. "Sorry, Doc, it just won't hold water. Okay—one more chance. Are you going to tell me what's really going on, or shall I tell Cristóbal to start swinging that whip?"

Doc sighed. "You're makin' a big mistake—"

"If I am, you're the one who suffers from it, not me. But I'm not an unreasonable man. Anytime you feel like talking, just holler out, and I'll listen. What could be fairer than that?"

Doc clamped his mouth shut tight and didn't answer. He was handy with words, and he'd used them more than once as a defensive weapon, but the only trouble with words was that they ran out on you sometimes. They'd run out now; there was nothing more he could say to put off the inevitable.

The first blow of the whip caught him by surprise, stinging his back with a searing line of fire. He'd meant to take it in silence—show Magrue what he was made of—but he cried out in pain involuntarily. A moment later there was a second blow, and then a third. He managed to grit his teeth against the third one, but he gritted them so hard that he bit his lip and blood trickled down the side of his chin.

"Better start talking, Doc," called Magrue. "We can keep this up all night if we have to."

A fourth blow—and a fifth. After six or maybe seven Doc began to lose count. The pain across his back was excruciating; his flesh must be starting to resemble raw meat. The pain was spreading nearly all over him; it was seeping into the marrow of his bones. There was a red film in front of his eyes, and the stone wall he faced was rocking back and forth in his vision. Somewhere in the midst of all this he heard Cristóbal grunting as he delivered the blows. Now he'd *really* lost count. Must have been a dozen or more by now. He heard wild laughter and thought it might be his own. Except it wasn't exactly laughter—there was a wail of pain and misery and despair in it somewhere. His legs were weak: he felt himself slipping, then hanging by the thongs that held his wrists to the iron bars above him.

"Not too fast, Cristóbal," Magrue's voice called, as though down a long tunnel. "Keep him awake."

Either Cristóbal disregarded the warning or Magrue gave it too late. The red film in front of Doc's eyes turned to gray, and a moment later it was black. Everything was black. Everything was nothing. If Doc had been able to realize it, he would have welcomed it. At least he no longer felt the pain.

Night fell again at Zama Pueblo, atop Spanish Rock. The stars were silver sequins in a blue-black sky, extending from one horizon to the other. Holding Raider's hand, Kara led him silently toward the western edge of the great rock, where the rugged cliff fell away more than three hundred feet almost straight down, as it did on all sides of the plateau.

The day, in Raider's estimation, had been rather dull and unproductive. The night before, at the meal they'd finally been served in the meeting hall, he'd felt the intoxication of the peyote and for a while had thought it quite possible he might end up in either Genevieve's or Kara's arms—whichever one of them circumstances led to. Circumstances, unfortunately, had turned out otherwise. Before long, Genevieve had become glassy-eyed from the peyote and had begun giggling uncontrollably. Finally, her father had escorted her to bed, with much sighing, after finding out where she was to be quartered. With Genevieve scratched, Raider had turned his attention to Kara. But she would not put her attention upon him. She was busy with her interpreting in the long pow-wow that followed. At last, when the chief seemed satisfied and appeared to be bringing the conference to an end, she slipped out of the room suddenly and did not return.

Raider followed one of the councilmen, who led him to a single room in another building, showing him the woven mat and blankets on which he was to sleep. By that time the effect of the peyote was wearing off, and, while he was normally horny—about like he always was—he wasn't so *damned* horny as he'd been a while ago. Not one to toss in his bed and stew when things weren't going exactly as he wished, he stretched himself out and fell asleep almost immediately, as he did on the trail with only the hard ground beneath him and a saddle for a pillow.

In the morning all the visitors were brought again to a meeting room, fed a breakfast of some kind of corn mush, and vaguely given to understand that they would spend the day exploring the village. It was difficult to say how this was communicated, for nothing to that effect was said directly, but somehow, by the time breakfast was finished, everyone understood that that was the plan. Kara was nowhere to be seen, and Joe Sunbird became their interpreter.

"But where's the chief?" Professor Ashley asked, looking around in his semibewildered way. "He's supposed to decide about showing us the artifacts, isn't he?"

"Hey, Professor," said Joe. "You take my advice, you don't push him, okay? He'll decide when one of his spirits or some goddamned thing tells him to."

"How can we be sure he'll ever decide?"

"No way to know. Maybe he's even gonna forget."

"Forget? What will happen then?"

"You just be shit out of luck, that's what happen," said Joe.

With some of the Indians walking them around the pueblo and showing them everything, it was like a guided tour on a canopied wagon, like they had in some cities, Raider decided. Maybe Doc would have enjoyed it if he'd been here, he thought; as for himself, well, all it did was make him yawn.

Genevieve seemed to take it all in with a certain amount of interest, if no outright pleasure. She watched as the morning work parties—mostly women—descended the rock to go down into the fields where the vegetable patches grew, irrigated by a nearby spring, and as some of the men, accompanied by scrawny dogs, rode off into the low hills to tend the herds of sheep. Each time an Indian returned from below, he or she brought back a jar of water, which held about three gallons, and dumped it into a reservoir on the plateau to replenish the supply.

"They like to keep lots on hand," Joe explained. "That way they can hold out if somebody tries to attack the goddamn place."

"Does that happen much?" Raider asked.

"Not these days. Used to be wars all the time. Now they just got the habit of bein' ready. And speakin' of water reminds me of whiskey, on account of they ain't at all alike. Professor, you forgot my bottle this mornin'."

"I thought that was only to be on the trail," said Ashley.

"Get just as goddamn thirsty up here as I do down there," said Joe.

"Oh, very well," said the professor, turning to head for his quarters. "But at this rate the supply won't last long."

"We'll worry about that when it runs out," said Joe. "That's one thing you gotta learn about this country. Today is today, tomorrow is tomorrow, no?"

"An interesting philosophy," said Ashley, moving off.

In mid-afternoon, as the group was moving about just as aimlessly, Raider lagged a little behind to watch one old Indian, squatting in the sun, his back against a bright adobe wall, attaching flint arrowheads to a number of shafts. The others were out of sight when he heard his name called behind him; he turned and saw Kara standing there.

Raider smiled. "Well, there you are. Where you been?"

Kara remained several feet from him and did not return his smile. "We must meet, Raider."

"Been thinkin' that," Raider said.

"Alone," she said.

"That's what I mean," said Raider.

"Be at the water trough tonight, just after sundown."

"Wild bulls couldn't keep me from it," said Raider, laughing softly.

She turned sharply, walked away, and disappeared around the corner of one of the sunbaked houses.

Here he was now, Kara leading him somewhere by the hand. He had started to greet her when he'd met her at the cistern, but she'd put her finger to her lips to admonish him to silence. He frowned a little in puzzlement. Somehow, she wasn't acting like a gal inviting him to a roll in the hay—or blanket, or mats, or whatever was customary here. He kept silent and went along with it.

Threading their way among the houses and chicken pens and sheep corrals, they emerged presently upon a stretch of flat rock beyond the village proper and kept going toward the cliff edge. In the starshine, Raider saw a small, low adobe structure ahead. Like all the houses, it had no doors in its sides but a ladder that led to the roof and the trapdoor there for access to the inside.

They climbed the ladder, found the trapdoor, and Kara descended, beckoning for him to follow. It was much darker inside, though some light came in from the trapdoor, especially now that the moon was beginning to rise. He blinked several times to accustom his eyes to the semidarkness and saw that they were in a small room in which a number of kegs, each a foot or so in diameter, were stacked against the walls.

Raider sniffed. "Gunpowder."

"Yes," said Kara. "We keep it here, away from the village."

"Smart way to do. Good place to come, too. We won't be bothered." He could feel her warmth and detect her sweet aura as she stood facing him; he could make out the outline of her trim figure in the dim light. He reached forward to put his hands on her waist and draw her toward him.

"No," she said, without drawing away, but in a firm tone of voice. "Not that."

"Not that? Look, I thought—"

"I know. I could see what you were thinking. I understand perfectly. But it is not why I brought you here."

"Why the hell did you, then?"

"It would be better if you would calm yourself," she said blandly.

"Okay, I'll simmer down. But it won't be easy."

"We will sit," she said. "We will talk."

"Goddamn," said Raider. "Here I am with a powerful appetite, and all I end up with is conversation."

"Please," said Kara. "This is of the greatest importance."

Following her lead, Raider lowered himself and squatted cross-legged on the floor, which, like all the floors in the houses here, was a hard compound of claylike soil and sheep blood. "Fire away," he said.

"You must know something first about our tribe, and about Tabaydeh, and about myself. Then I will explain what Tabaydeh wishes to convey to you—and you will understand it much better."

"I'm listening," said Raider.

"We are the Zama. In our particular language—which we use now mainly in ceremonies—that means simply 'The People.' It expresses what we feel: that we are at the center of everything and that all others, while they are, of course, people, are of lesser importance. Such an attitude is found in any social group, although perhaps not as strongly as it is with us."

"Look, Kara," said Raider, smiling a little. "This kinda talk would go better with the professor. He goes in for things like this—has lots of big words for what plain folks know just by common sense."

"Still, you must hear me out. So that everything is quite clear. And Tabaydeh said you were the one to talk to. He senses that you are the leader."

"Hadn't thought about that." Raider shrugged. "Well, anyway, go ahead."

"The first thing you should know is that what the professor seeks is here. I can tell you at least that much, though I'm not ready yet to show you exactly where it is. Should you be evil of heart, in spite of Tabaydeh's belief that you are not, and

wish to take these things by force—either now or
by returning later—I assure you that you, or anyone else, will find it impossible to locate them. At
the very worst, we would destroy everything before
you could lay your hands on it."

"Let's get something straight right now," said
Raider. "Personally, I don't give a hoot about the
professor's pots and pans. But I don't mind givin'
him a hand in finding them, because it fits in with
a couple of other things I have to do. Never mind
just now what they are. Maybe you'll learn later,
and maybe you won't. Anyway, rest easy. Nobody's
gonna steal the damn things from you."

"That is what we hoped," said Kara, and he saw
her nod. "Though it's true there is much of great
value in the artifacts."

"So I heard. More than the professor thought,
according to an old Spanish gent in Tesqua—Don
Luis Mondragon. We're still not stealing anything.
That just ain't the way we operate. You see, what
the professor has in mind is not to take anything
you don't want to give, but maybe borrow some of
it, or, at the very least, make a bunch of notes and
sketches on the stuff to take back with him."

"Very well," said Kara, nodding. "It seems that
we have something you wish. It would be only fair
that we trade for something *we* wish."

"That makes sense. Okay, what do you want?"

"You have mentioned Seth Magrue, the Indian
agent. You must be familiar with what he is doing."

"Got a line on it," said Raider cautiously.

"Well, it's very simple, then. We wish to have
Seth Magrue removed."

"Removed?"

"All right, I will say it honestly. He must be
killed."

Raider's eyebrows rose. "That *is* sayin' it right out. Killed, huh? Got any idea how, and who's gonna do it?"

"Tabaydeh thinks you might be the one. He says when he looks in your eyes he knows you are a man who will kill when it is necessary. More than that, he believes you know how to do it, and do it well."

"Dally in here, just a moment. This is goin' by too fast," said Raider. "First, if you people want Magrue killed, how come you haven't just gone ahead and done it?"

"All the tribes would like to see him dead, not only ourselves, the Zama. But there are two reasons the attempt has never been made, though I assure you it's been discussed more than once. For one thing, he keeps himself well guarded. For another, it would be very difficult for an Indian to do it with any secrecy. The actual perpetrator might not be identified, but everyone would be sure to know it was the work of an Indian. This would bring the federal government down upon us, and even the fact that Magrue had been cheating the Indians wouldn't lessen the consequences. If, however, Magrue were killed by a white man, it would never be connected to the Indians, and he'd be replaced by a new agent—one, we hope, who wouldn't cheat us."

Raider was silent for several long moments, thinking. "I'll tell you, Kara," he said finally. "I got no use for Magrue and would as lief see him in West Hell as anyplace else. But when you come to me, you're barkin' up the wrong tree. The chief's right—I can use a gun, and I have, lots of times, in self-defense. I just don't hire out my gun, that's all. It ain't my profession."

"I am sorry to hear that," said Kara.

He smiled at her in the darkness. "All that schooling back east didn't make you so damned civilized, after all, did it?"

"What do you mean by that?"

"Well, you talk just like a fine lady, and I'll bet you know which silverware to use at a dinner party. But down deep you're ready to kill."

"In self-defense!" she said hotly. "The same as you have."

"Maybe. Just the same, you're what some folks'd call 'savage' inside. I ain't faultin' you for it—just stating a fact."

"Raider—" she said in a quieter voice.

"Yeah?"

"You don't know how it is inside me. You don't know the agony of it."

"What agony?"

"I will tell you a tale of these conquistadores the professor seems to admire so much. It is told in our kiva, when we talk to all the spirits, along with many other tales handed down from generation to generation. It seems that when these soldiers of Coronado wished to punish someone—either Indian or one of their own kind—they would sometimes play tug-of-war with him. They would lead ropes from both his arms and legs, and men would pull from either side until the line was crossed. It was a game, and there was much laughter. So much for the civilized instincts of the white man. At any rate, I feel like that person in the tug-of-war. Pulled from both sides, wondering when I'm going to be torn apart."

"Pulled by what?"

"By the white man's ways—which I've learned well—and by the ways of my Indian ancestors, which are still strong in my heart. Sometimes I don't know who I am, or what I must be."

"Reckon you've got a problem there," said Raider. "Damned if I know what you can do about it. Maybe you should just leave—go back east again. Things might be easier all around. Folks back there maybe want to kill somebody, just like folks everywhere do, once in a while, but they're not usually so quick to do it. Could be there's not so much opportunity for it."

She shook her head. "I will not return. I have promised Tabaydeh I will stay. Besides, my place is here."

He shrugged. "If that's how you see it. But all you got here for your future is to be a toothless old squaw gummin' on mocassin leather to make it soft someday. While your husband goes out and hunts and gets drunk and has all the fun. Come to think of it, how come you didn't marry up with anybody yet?"

"That is another curse I've acquired from the white man's world. Here, your mate is chosen for you when you are still a child. None was chosen for me because I was away most of the time. But in the white man's society one *finds* his or her mate —falls in love, as they say. This idea has crept into my heart. I cannot bring myself to marry unless there is love—though I'm not sure precisely what love is. At any rate, nothing like that has ever come along."

Raider cocked his head. "Don't tell me you never, uh, you know."

"Oh, I've played at making love, if that's what you mean. I am not a virgin. If one of our women is still a virgin at fourteen, that is a disgrace. Does that shock your civilized sensibilities?"

"Hardly," said Raider. "Sounds like a good idea." He reached out and put his hands on her shoulders. "That bein' the case," he said, "what are we waitin' for?"

She fumbled quickly to remove her velvet bodice and the Spanish blouse beneath it. Raider just as hastily began to divest himself of his own clothing. In moments, he could see her slim, naked body in diffused outline in the semidarkness. Her breasts were small but firm, their hard little nipples pouting upward. Her legs were supple and invitingly parted. As he sat there, his own stretched out before him, she forked herself upon his thighs and lowered herself gently upon his great, hardened dong, letting it seek the warm slash of her quim in its triangular nest of dark hair. He penetrated hard and deep, the tip of his penis reaching a resilient wall inside, giving her what must have been a touch of pain, for she gasped with it. But in that gasp, and in the moan that followed, there was also a note of the greatest joy and ecstasy.

Gently, then, both rolled upon their sides, and Raider began to thrust in and out with increasing tempo. Her moans turned into an almost continuous murmur of delight. She brought her mouth to his ear, breathed hot breath into it, then darted her tongue inside. Her fingernails dug into Raider's muscular back as she clasped him tightly. He rolled atop her then, kept thrusting, and presently rolled her to her other side. Around and around, they gyrated that way, their pelvises smashing together with each stroke, so that at times they seemed to be submerged in some great, green sea instead of rolling on a hard adobe floor.

She bit his neck. Hard.

"See what I mean?" he muttered, half in jest. "Still a savage."

"Yes, yes!" she cried. "Oh, Raider—make me crazy with it!"

He did his best.

Overhead, in the trapdoor, the moon crossed the clear, starry sky and stared imperturbably into the little room, as Raider and Kara satisfied themselves over and over again.

CHAPTER ELEVEN

In a way, Doc didn't want to wake up, because with wakefulness came the terrible pain. There was a gray dawn outside, and he lay on the floor of the cell. He lay flat on his stomach and knew that it was well he did, for if he had been on his back the raw lacerations upon it would have glued him to the floor, and that would have been even more painful—if it was possible that anything could be more painful than what he felt now.

He ground his teeth together and breathed deeply in an effort to contain the pain. His cheek to the cold floor, he looked toward the bars of the cell and tried to distract himself by taking in the room beyond it. Magrue, Busby, and Cristóbal were gone. In the room, his back partly turned as he sat at the sheriff's rolltop desk, was Cristóbal's thin and grimy sidekick, Transito. He had a checkerboard on the desk and, with great concentration and sometimes muttering softly in Spanish, was evidently playing a game against himself, occasionally trying out moves, then taking them back again when they didn't satisfy him.

Doc watched awhile, then said, "Who's winning?"

Transito turned his head and stared at Doc stupidly. "Eh?"

"I said, 'Who's winning?' "

Transito thought for a moment, then said, "I am. *Naturalmente.*"

"Where's everybody?"

"*Que?* Where is who?"

128

"Okay, they're off somewhere. They left you here to guard me, right?"

"Don't try any tricks," said Transito, scowling.

"What tricks? I'm just making conversation. Long as we're both here, we might as well talk. Passes the time, huh?"

"*Quizás,*" said Transito. "Maybe."

"Didn't know you were a jailer," said Doc. "Good job?"

"I don't know what you're talking about. And dont get no ideas, no? I'm keeping an eye on you, gringo."

"Sure. That's what a jailer's supposed to do. Also, he's supposed to take care of the prisoners. How about a drink of water?"

"Eh?"

"Water. *Agua.*"

"Okay," said Transito, scowling even more deeply. "I get you some water." He crossed the room to the upended bottle with its spigot and thumbed water into a not very clean tumbler. He came to the bars of the cell and held out the water, his hand between the bars.

"I can't get up to get it," said Doc. "You can see that."

"I no coming in there," said Transito, shaking his head.

Doc tried not to show his disappointment. Not that he was sure that in his weakened condition, he could take Transito if the man came near him, but, what the hell, it was worth a try. With great effort, he pushed himself upward and staggered to his feet. New pains shot through the raw slashes on his back. He swayed for a moment, adjusting himself to the agony, then came forward to where Transito still held the glass of water ready. Trying not to move his eyes too obviously, he took in Transito, noting details. Six-gun on his hip, for one thing. That showed right there he wasn't much of a jailer; it was basic that you didn't approach a prisoner with arms where he might reach them. And there was one mistake—one Doc had hoped for. The key to the cell, an oversized hunk of iron, hung by a string from a wooden tab Transito had thrust into his belt.

Raider sometimes told Doc he talked too much, and maybe so, but this was one time when talk was useful. It would distract Transito, as a prestidigitator distracts an onlooker by making busy motions with the hand that isn't doing anything.

Moving slowly toward the extended glass of water, as though the pain kept him from going too quickly—which, as a matter of fact, it did—Doc began his spiel. Didn't make much difference what he said, as long as he kept it up and held Transito's attention. "Looks like Magrue really trusts you, eh, Transito? You must be a pretty important man in his outfit. Leaving you here like this to stand guard. Of course, I can understand he couldn't use any of his regular deputies, 'cause he's holding me here without charges, and that there's kinda illegal. Not that I expect they'd mind too much, but he must figure it's better all around to have an important man like yourself do the job, right?"

"I don't know," said Transito, holding his scowl. "I just know I'm gonna keep you here, gringo, so you better be careful."

"Well, I can see you're not such a bad hombre, after all," said Doc cheerfully. "Sure appreciate the *agua*, the way I'm feelin' here."

"Okay, okay, take it," said Transito impatiently.

Doc moved swiftly. His hand, snaking forward, grabbed not the water but Transito's wrist. The tumbler fell to the floor of the cell and broke. All together, as though in one motion, Doc twisted the jailer's arm upward and outward, and his other hand flashed through the bars to the six-gun at Transito's side. Transito had just time enough to grunt sharply with pain from his twisted arm, and then Doc had the muzzle of the gun to his temple.

"Hey, Transito," he said, grinning coldly. "I'll tell you something now. I'm not a nice, kind hombre the way you are. I wouldn't mind blowing your brains all over this room at all. In fact, I'd kinda enjoy it."

"Madre de Dios, señor!" said Transito. "Don' do that!"

"The key, Transito. Throw it on the floor in here."

"Si! Si! Don't shoot!" Transito's eyes rolled wildly. Still grimacing with the pain in his bent arm, he reached down with his other hand, took the wooden tab from his belt, and tossed it as Doc had directed.

Doc pushed him off. "Stay right where you are!" he said. "You move, and I'll put a bullet right in your *panza."*

Congratulating himself that so far it had been easier than he'd expected, Doc presently was out of the cell and, with the gun, was gesturing Transito into it. He eyed the scrawny, unkempt *bandido* for a moment and considered trying to bind and gag him, then realized that that would give *him* a chance to make a counterplay and decided not to press his luck.

"Face the wall, Transito," said Doc in a disarmingly even tone of voice.

Transito turned. Immediately Doc brought the butt of the Colt .45 down on Transito's head. Hard. But not *too* hard. The idea was to put him to sleep awhile, not to kill him. Hitting him just right called for finesse—like making a difficult bank shot at the pool table. That was something Doc had plenty of—finesse—though there were times when Raider didn't seem to appreciate it.

He leaned over Transito, who was now slumped on the floor, touched his neck, felt a pulse, and nodded in satisfaction at his handiwork. Before he closed and locked the cell door, Doc slipped on his shirt and pearl-gray vest, wincing as the cloth rubbed on the lacerations across his back. He'd better get goose grease on those pretty soon, he told himself, maybe with some carbolic acid mixed in the wagon, but the wagon was locked and parked near the livery stable, and he wasn't sure he could get to it unseen. What he needed was to get out of town as fast as possible so he could breathe easier —and then think a little more about his predica- ment. A horse, that was what he needed. Plenty of horses around, no doubt, but not so many folks who'd want to lend him one. For that, he'd need somebody friendly. Somebody who'd keep his mouth shut, too, after Doc disappeared and high- tailed it for Spanish Rock to find Raider. Don Luis? A possibility, though it was a long walk without much concealment out to his hacienda.

He opened the door cautiously and peered out into the street. Empty. He'd figured it might be, this early in the morning. He tiptoed out of the office and then started down the walkway under the *portales* that lined this side of the plaza. A dog came waggling from the cactus garden in the cen- ter of the plaza and, in puppyish exuberance, started to jump at Doc, inviting him to play. "God- damn it, not now, fella!" said Doc. "Vamoose!"

The puppy scurried off.

Doc, keeping close to the walls, was hurrying to

get away from the plaza, where someone who oughtn't to see him might appear at any moment, when a sleek white horse clattered onto the square from the main road. A moment later he recognized its slim rider in her Spanish pants and broad dish-brimmed hat. Forgetting caution for the moment, he dashed across the park area to the entrance to the posada, where she was dismounting.

"Susanita!"

She turned and stared at him.

"It's me—Doc! I need some help!"

She clicked toward him in her high-heeled riding boots. Admiring her lithe, trim figure, Doc imagined Raider must have had a pretty good time with her; he wouldn't mind trying out something like that himself. But that, at the moment, was kinda beside the point.

"Where have you been? What's happened to you?" She was still staring in astonishment.

"No time to explain. Magrue had me in the pokey—I just got out. Look, I need a horse. How about yours?"

"To go where?"

"The hell out of here. As far as I can."

"Doc, I'm sorry. You can't take Brujo. Everybody would wonder—ask questions."

"Then get me another one, okay? Any old nag you can find, as long as it moves. And get me off the street here, fast, before one of Magrue's men sees me."

Susanita needed only a fraction of a second to assess the situation. She nodded then. "Meet me around the corner—under that old cottonwood. There's a firewood bin there you can hide behind. I have business in the inn—papers Don Luis wants me to deliver to someone. I'll only be a few minutes."

Doc nodded. "See you then. If I'm still all in one piece."

She continued on to the inn, and Doc, still keeping in what shadow there was close to the wall, walked swiftly from the plaza, turned right on the main street, and, seeing no one about, ran the rest of the way to the old cottonwood.

He found the firewood bin and crouched behind it. The shirt and vest he was wearing had rubbed some of the clotted blood from the gashes on his back, and they were hurting again like the very devil. He considered removing them, but then decided he needed to keep clothed against the morning chill—it was always a little nippy at this high altitude before the sun really started climbing.

He didn't care for waiting like this, scrunched down behind the wattled bin with its load of pinyon logs, but at least it gave him a chance to dally a spell and think things out. First thing to do was put distance between himself and Magrue. Next thing was to ride like hell and make Spanish Rock as fast as he could, if he had to drop a horse in its tracks to do it. After that, he'd warn Raider that Magrue now had a pretty good idea of what they were up to, even though he wasn't sure of the details. And after that he wasn't sure what they ought to do—Raider would no doubt have an idea or two, and, between them, they'd come up with something, the way they always did.

Bitterly, he wondered if Raider had managed to make it under Genevieve's petticoats by now. He'd be in there trying—that was for sure. The bastard. Though, come to think of it, Doc, who had no intention of making any kind of permanent liaison with Genevieve, delightful as she was, also had no right to be jealous of her. Well, right be damned. He *was* jealous—couldn't stand the thought of

Raider dipping that big wick in his own personal property. If it turned out he had, Doc would probably take a swing at him and they'd have another of their knock-down-and-drag-out brawls. But that'd be after they'd dealt with Magrue. Together, the way they always did.

He heard a horse clatter up to the cottonwood just beyond the bin. Bringing his head carefully around the side of the box, he saw Susanita on the white stallion. She did not have a second mount with her; her own was sidestepping a bit, as stallions do, and she was holding it more or less in place with the reins. "On his back," she said quickly, pointing to the creature's rump behind the saddle. "As quickly as you can!"

Doc ran forward, then vaulted onto the horse, grabbing Susanita to steady himself and, by accident, putting his hands on her resilient breasts. The marvelous feel of them almost made him forget what he was doing. But there was a time and a place for everything, and this was neither for whatever ideas the feel of her breasts was giving him.

The stallion reared as Doc jumped upon it, and Susanita fought it for a moment to bring it down again. He had no doubt she could handle a man the way she handled a horse, if she had a mind to.

She wheeled the horse, gave it its head, and let it break into a canter, Doc still clinging to her, his unstirruped legs flailing wildly on the creature's flanks. She turned it abruptly onto the road that led out to Don Luis's hacienda, and they galloped forward on the huge steed, clouds of dust rising behind them.

"Better'n I hoped," said Doc, jolting out the words between bounces. "I was figurin' on makin' my way out to the hacienda."

"We're not going there," she said, twisting her head a little so he could hear her. "Another place. Where you'll find a horse."

"Okay, whatever you say," said Doc. "Long as I can get goin' pretty damn pronto."

Moments later another turnoff led down a rutted side road to a small sheep raiser's *jacale* beside a small barn and a corral. In one place the top rail of the fence was slanting down, and the stallion leapt it with both people on him. Doc almost lost his hold and fell off when he came down again. Then Susanita forced the beast to a halt in front of the barn, and Doc slipped from its back. With the creature still refusing to stay perfectly still, its eyes wild and its nostrils flaring, Susanita, needing both hands on the reins, nodded at the barn and said, "In there. Take what you need. The owner's not here, but I'll explain to him afterward. It'll be all right. He's a friend."

"Much thanks!" said Doc. "Maybe I can repay you one of these days."

"Perhaps. Though I don't need it. What you can do is tell me how and why you ended up in the jail."

"No time for the whole story," said Doc. "To make it short, Magrue got suspicious of me and Raider, followed me to Santa Fe, caught me off guard, and dragged me here."

"I don't understand. Suspicious of what?"

"You might as well know, since you and Don Luis are against Magrue, anyway. Raider and I work for the Pinkerton Agency. We were sent here to look into the way Magrue's stealin' the Indians blind. Well, we got an idea how he does it now, but we're still gonna have to go some to pin it on him. Even if we don't, it won't be long till he's out on his ear, once they get our report. I reckon Don Luis'll be glad to hear that."

"But what about Spanish Rock? Why did you start out for there?"

"Just makin' things look natural. And gettin' away, so's we could operate. Like I say, no time to explain all the details. So thanks again. We'll be back before long—I know Raider's lookin' forward to seeing you again. Hell," he added, grinning, "so am I!"

"Get your horse, Doc," she said, nodding again at the barn. "Ride."

"Sure will. Adios."

He knew that she was still there, astride the stallion, as he stepped toward the barn. He patted the gun he'd taken from Transito to make sure it was still in his belt and hadn't jolted loose during the wild ride. He might need it to get himself some food on his way to Spanish Rock—a jackrabbit, maybe, even if they were tough and tasted strong. Not a prairie dog, anyway. Raider was right about the sonsabitches—they could see and duck bullets.

A smaller door was in the big swinging doors of the barn. He opened it. He took one step inside.

Men converged on him from either side, grabbed him, pinioned his arms, and then someone struck him over the head with a pistol butt, missing the mark a little so that he didn't black out but his legs wobbled and he almost fell.

After he had blinked several times he realized that he was once more in the company of Seth Magrue, Sheriff Busby, and the toadlike bandit, Cristóbal.

Magrue, striking a pose with his hands on his hips, ran a palm over his completely bald head, returned his hand to his hip, then grinned icily at Doc. "Thanks for the information, Doc," he said.

"I figured you'd give it to Susanita quicker than you would to us!"

Doc was flabbergasted. For once, he couldn't find words right away. "You mean—you—she—?"

"Exactly," said Magrue. "A setup right from the start. Not a bad one, if I say so myself. Of course, Transito didn't expect to get himself cold-cocked, but I imagine he'll get over it."

The stallion's hooves sounded behind him again; Doc turned and saw Susanita, at the door now, looking down at him and smiling a little, but with a smile that had no friendliness in it, whatsoever. "Doc," she said, "you can tell Raider when you see him that the score is even. You can tell him that *no* man can refuse what Susanita offers and be unpunished for it!"

"What the hell are you talkin' about?" asked Doc helplessly.

"Raider will know," she said grimly. "He will know very well."

She whirled the stallion and rode off at a hard gallop, plumes of dust rising behind her.

Busby and Cristóbal now grabbed Doc roughly, the sheriff yanking the pistol from his belt and throwing it into the hay and manure that covered the floor of the barn. They shoved him against a stall fence, and Cristóbal picked up a pitchfork and held it with its glistening prongs extended toward Doc.

"Well, here we all are again," said Magrue. "Very cozy when old friends get together. And you'll be happy to hear, Doc, that we won't require you to do a lot of talking this time. That's because, thanks to Susanita, we've got all the information we need."

"You mean she's been in cahoots with you all the time?"

"Well, not until just recently, actually. Seems your friend Raider spurned her or something. Can't imagine why he did—there's a piece no man should turn down, especially if it throws itself right at him. Anyway, to get back at Raider, she came to me and told me what you two and the professor were really after out there at Spanish Rock. Not just old armor and cooking utensils, eh, Doc? Gold and jewels, like Don Luis's family records say. She knew that'd interest me, and that chances were I'd have to take care of Raider in order to latch on to such a treasure. The beauty of it was that her showing up like that fitted itself neatly into everything else. Here you were, hanging tough, not talking. Got to hand it to you, Doc —you can take it. But I knew you'd talk to Susanita, so I arranged everything so you could. Far be it from me to gloat, Doc, but the fact is you and Raider bit off more than you could chew when you started tangling with Seth Magrue."

"All right, Magrue. You won a round. What's next?"

"More than a round, Doc," said Magrue, obviously relishing his moment of triumph. "The fight's over. Finished. *You're* finished, Doc. Raider's next, but you're already finished."

"And what's that supposed to mean?"

"Come now, Doc, you're not so stupid that you can't guess. Put yourself in my position. Do you think I could let you go, just to wander off and start blabbing somewhere, with all you know? I must admit that I'd rather not have all the trouble of disposing of persons, but I'm afraid you leave me no choice. Well, how do you feel? Scared?"

"Goddamn right I am!" said Doc. "What do you think I am, superhuman?"

"The way you and Raider have been acting I

wouldn't be surprised to learn you did regard your-selves along those lines. But everything comes to an end, Doc, and I presume you're beginning to understand that now. You know, Doc, we're alike in some ways, you and Raider and I. When we want something we don't let anything stand in our way, and when we act, it's quick and hard and fast and able. It puts us a cut above most men, and there's no point in being falsely modest and deny-ing it. I made myself what I am, and it wasn't easy. I grew up in an orphan home, Doc, so poor a mouse was rich compared to me, and one hell of a lot less miserable. I told myself I'd never be that way again, and, by God, that's how it's worked out. The only way to get anywhere is to take what you want, by any means you can." He laughed abruptly. "I'm wasting time with all this."

"Suits me," said Doc. "Keep talkin'."

Magrue shook his head. "Too much to be done. You see, Doc, much as I'd like to simplify matters, I can't just put a bullet in you and drop your body off somewhere. Too much chance you'd be missed and other investigators would come smelling around. It's got to be an accident, Doc; one that looks good and makes 'em shrug and say, 'Too bad about old Doc,' and then forget it."

"Which they might not do. They might look into an accident, too."

"I doubt it. At any rate, it's my best bet right now. Good try, Doc, but I'm afraid it's too late for that golden tongue of yours to talk me out of any-thing."

"Now, hold on a minute, Magrue," said Doc, trying hard not to let his voice show the despera-tion that was gnawing at him inside. "Has it oc-curred to you you might be goin' off half-cocked? You don't know Raider and me—I mean, what

we're really like. You said we're like you in some
ways, and you hit the nail on the head there.
Pinkerton don't pay us all that much, in either
money or respect, that we can't look out for ourselves, if need be. So what if we started thinkin'
about ourselves and kind of worked *with* you instead of lockin' horns, the way we been doin'?"

Magrue laughed. "Doc, those are words of a man
backed into a corner—way up a creek and up to
his ass in alligators. Can't blame you; I'd make a
try like that myself if I were in your shoes. Anything to put it off, eh, Doc? Hoping you'll get out
of it somehow, when you know damn well, in your
heart, you can't. Well, if it makes you feel better,
you just go ahead and hope. Meanwhile, time's
up." He glanced at Sheriff Busby and Cristóbal.
"Horses ready?"

Busby had been eating pinyon nuts out of his
sack. "Out back," he said, angling his head.

"Good. Let's go," said Magrue.

By taking back roads and cutting across several
fields, the small procession went unseen. Magrue
led the way; Busby and Cristóbal positioned themselves on either side of Doc. Doc, his wrists bound
behind him, his arms further pinioned to his sides
by coils of three-eighths lariat line, was on a sway-
backed, hook-nosed old spotted gelding they'd
found somewhere, and Magrue, leading the horse,
was cursing and yanking at his mouth to get him
to move at a slow walk so he could keep pace with
the others. Evidently the gelding's mouth had been
yanked all his life, and he no longer cared about
the pain and discomfort.

"Caballo estupido!" said Cristóbal, spitting at
him. "If a snail come along, he gonna pass you!"

"Shut up and keep riding," Magrue called back. "We got a ways to go yet."

Presently they were in the rolling, clump-dotted desert beyond the town, and Doc rode silently, twisting his hands and fumbling with his fingers behind him in an effort to work his bonds loose, getting nowhere with this and sadly realizing it. What ranchitos they passed on the way out were in the distance, though Doc stared at those he saw and mentally grasped at wild schemes to attract someone's attention. Hurt and startle the old gelding, maybe, so he'd break into a crazy gallop, Doc forking hard with his thighs to stay on him. Talk Magrue into resting a spell and somehow start a fire. Or kick their weapons away with his feet and then fight 'em that way, like a Frenchman. Nothing he thought of was very practical.

In the top of his mind he knew he was about to die, but in the bottom of his mind it just didn't seem real to him. He wished Raider were here. He'd like to show the sonofabitch how he could die like a man, if he had to.

The sun was high by the time they came to the gorge of the Brazos, riding up to it suddenly, so that if it had been night they might have tumbled right into it. Magrue called a halt at the lip of the gorge. He and the others dismounted. Doc shifted uncomfortably in the saddle and said, "Hey, how about me?"

"You're staying right where you are," Magrue said, with a hard smile.

"Goddamn!" said Doc. "If you're gonna kill me off, like you say, you can at least see to it I'm comfortable!"

"Take a look at the gorge, Doc," said Magrue, pulling the stubborn horse a little closer to it with great difficulty. "I brought you here because I happen to know this particular spot. See how it drops off? A good hundred feet, straight down. The river's just a little trickle now, so what you'll hit is rocks. Ever see a horse and rider after they've dropped that far? They go *splat!* and turn to jelly."

Doc stared at the gorge and then at Magrue again. "Magrue you—you wouldn't!"

"Wouldn't hell," said Magrue. "I'm about to. And after a while somebody'll see the buzzards and come along to investigate, and then they'll find you. And everybody'll say, 'What a shame poor old Doc rode too close to the edge and slipped.' They'll say good things about you at the funeral, like they always do. I'll see you have a nice one."

"You son of a bitch!" said Doc.

"Under the circumstances," said Magrue, "I think I can let those fighting words pass this time."

He turned again to Busby and Cristóbal. The fat sheriff was rubbing his rump after the long ride, and fumbling with his other hand to bring his sack of pinyon nuts out of his pocket. When he was less than comfortable, like this, his lips went into a little pout that made him look more than ever like a spoiled infant. "Now, listen to what I've got to say, you two," Magrue said, "so you get everything straight and do it right. This is supposed to be an accident, so it won't do for them to find him tied up the way he is. That means he's got to be untied, which he can't be for long—too chancy. So sheriff, you take most of the ropes off till you've got them down to a slipknot, which'll still hold him. And when I say go, Cristóbal, you give that sorry excuse for a horse the hardest whack you can—cut a switch from that pinyon tree over there. That way, the critter goes over the edge before Doc can do anything."

Cristóbal looked blank. "How you know that horse is gonna go over?"

"You hit him hard enough, he will. That's why I got a stupid one. All right, let's stop asking so many questions and get to it."

Drawing his knife, Cristóbal waddled off to cut a switch from the stunted, twisted tree. Busby, a great frown of concentration on his face, began to fumble with the ropes that held Doc's wrists.

Doc, still astride the spavined old cayuse, was high enough to look over the lip of the gorge and see part of the bottom. Magrue had said the river was just a trickle, and maybe it was, compared to its usual state, but it looked more than a few feet deep to him. The current was swift, and there was some white water around a few scattered rocks here and there, but it still looked almost deep enough to dive into. Hard to say exactly, of course, but there was at least a chance of that, in Doc's estimation. The only trouble was, the river was some distance out from the foot of the cliff, and to reach it, a man would have to take one hell of a run and arc himself into the air. Even then, he couldn't be sure of it, but that, with its odds of maybe a hundred to one, was the only chance left to him. He'd probably hit the rocks, damn it, but at least he'd go out trying. Which, in a way, was bravado, but in another way wasn't. He was still scared, just as Magrue had mentioned. Scared shitless, if the truth be known.

Busby had his bonds loose now, except for a tight loop, which he held taut, as though he'd just roped a calf. Cristóbal was coming up behind with a long, thick, twisted branch in his hand.

Something about all this just wasn't the way Doc would have expected it. What the hell was it? Ah, he had it. When a man was about to die his whole life was supposed to pass before his eyes. That wasn't happening. All he felt was numb, stupid. And still scared.

"Go!" cried Magrue.

Simultaneously, Cristóbal slammed the horse on its rump with the branch and Busby pulled the slipknot by the loop he'd put in the eye-hitch for just that purpose. His arms free, Doc braced himself to push as hard as he could when the horse went over, so he'd sail over its head and maybe, just maybe, make it to the water instead of the rocks.

The old horse was either more stupid or one hell of a lot smarter than they'd thought. Doc didn't have time to figure out which. Instead of plunging forward wildly when he was struck, like any horse in its right mind might be expected to do, the critter actually backed up, kicking with his hind feet at the unseen source of the sudden blow. All Doc could decide was that the beast must have had some mule in him, biologically impossible be damned.

"Hit him again!" Magrue was roaring, waving his arms at Cristóbal excitedly.

Even as Magrue was fussing this way and both Cristóbal and the fat sheriff were momentarily immobilized, unable to realize immediately what had gone wrong, Doc moved. The instant his hands were free he threw himself from the horse and to one side. In the confusion, that put the horse between him and Magrue and the sheriff, with the toadlike Cristóbal to the rear, trying to back away from the animal. There were now perhaps ten yards or a bit less between Doc and the edge of the drop. He propelled himself forward with all the speed he could put into his churning legs, and when he reached the lip of the gorge he leapt forward, curving out and away through the air in a deliberate dive.

The sensation of falling caught him in the pit of his stomach as he plummeted downward. It was intensified as he somersaulted in midair, unable to keep himself in a stable position. Although only a second or two passed during his descent, it felt as though it were much longer, and that time had been frozen thick till it flowed like molasses. His turn half-completed, he was near the bottom now, falling feet-first. There was roiling, humpbacked muddy water just below him—as he'd so desperately hoped to do, he'd cleared the rocks at the base of the drop.

He struck the water with terrible force, which surprised hell out of him because the last time he'd touched it water had been soft. The shock was like a sudden explosion that blew his wits apart. There was a stab of pain, though he wasn't sure quite where. In his legs where they struck, maybe, or maybe just all over him. He was engulfed by a curious numbness that wasn't exactly unconsciousness but wasn't being awake, either. In some way he knew he was underwater and being carried forward by the churning river, but in another way it all seemed a bad dream that couldn't possibly be happening. There was only one thing that kept him hanging on to life, and that was the knowledge that he *was* still alive.

CHAPTER TWELVE

Raider was getting restless. Except for his most pleasant affair with Kara, nothing was happening here at the Zama Pueblo atop Spanish Rock, out in the desert, way beyond hell and gone. The hours in the sun, and under the crystal-cut stars at night, were passing as they had passed here for centuries, as though time in this world moved sideways instead of forward and could neither be measured nor counted.

They were all still waiting for Tabaydeh's decision as to whether or not to show them the artifacts—which, they were now convinced, were definitely here—but the old chief was keeping himself scarce, and they glimpsed him only occasionally as they wandered, more or less aimlessly, through the village and across the plateau on which it lay.

Raider, the professor, Genevieve, and Joe Sunbird squatted by a beehive oven to engage, by mutual consent, in what amounted to a council of war. They hadn't specifically planned to talk this way; they had somehow just naturally drifted into it.

Joe Sunbird tilted a pint bottle and drained what little was left in it. He regarded the empty vessel quizzically with his unpatched eye, then dropped it aside with a gesture that reflected both his disappointment and his resignation to it. "Professor, you sure this here's the last one?"

"Quite sure. I had no idea we'd be here this long."

"Shee-yit!" said Joe, disgustedly.

Raider looked at him with a half smile. "You might try some of that beer, or whatever it is, they make here."

"I'd as soon drink hog swill," said Joe.

"It's very interesting," said the professor, "how all primitive peoples make a form of beer. The ancient Babylonians had it as early as 6000 B.C."

"Fuck the Babylonians," said Joe.

Raider cleared his throat, frowned at Joe, glanced at Genevieve, then swung the frown back to Joe again. He didn't insist on delicate talk only in the presence of ladies, especially when it was artificial, as so many polite customs were, but it had to be said that Joe *was* overdoing it a bit. Genevieve caught his glance, smiled, and said, "It's all right, Raider. If I'm going to be out here, where things are a bit rough, I'll simply have to get used to it. Which, as a matter of fact, I'm doing."

"Well," said Raider, "be that as it may, the fact is we're gettin' nowhere here at the pueblo. I don't know what the hell's goin' on in the chief's mind, or why he even lets us stay and treats us pretty good if he doesn't mean to show us that old Spanish stuff, but, then, Indian thinkin' is about the one thing I never *could* figure out exactly."

"Heard all that before," said Joe, spitting to one side. "What the white man can't see is that the Indian don't ever go *through* the bush, he goes *around* it. And when you think about it, goin' around's a lot less trouble."

"An excellent assessment!" said the professor, delighted.

Raider sighed. "Well, what it all boils down to is we're not gettin' what we came here for. And I'm wastin' *my* time out here, too."

Genevieve looked at him closely. Raider had thought that fair skin of hers would turn red in all this sun, but it was tanning nicely instead, and looking real good against her pale blond hair. He reflected again how well stacked she was, and wondered, as always, if he'd ever get around to making it with her. If Kara hadn't been around to help him let off some of the steam, he'd be trying harder with Genevieve—as much for the chance to show Doc up as for the sake of the conquest itself.

Genevieve said, "Raider, you hinted before that you were more than just a purveyor of medicines. But we still don't know what you're really up to."

"Can't tell you everything," said Raider, shaking his head. "Let's just let things ride the way they are, okay?"

"It involves Magrue, doesn't it?"

"Maybe. Forget the questions. I ain't gonna answer. What I'm thinkin' about now is what we ought to do. Looks like you might be here a month of Sundays before the chief shows you anything— and maybe he'll decide against it even then. Anyway, why *should* he show you the artifacts? What good does it do him or the tribe to let the world know about what he's got?"

Joe Sunbird looked up from under the brim of his broad hat. "There you go thinkin' he thinks like a white man again. You listen to me, goddamn it, *primo*, 'cause I know both ways o' thinkin'. And I been keepin' my ears and my one good eye open around here, so I know how the Zama are lookin' at everything. The chief's got two things he wants pullin' at him, and he can't decide which, that's all."

"I don't follow you," said Raider.

"You shut up awhile and let me talk and maybe you can," said Joe.

"Go ahead," said Raider, grinning.

"First," said Joe, "he wants attention from the outside, so's somebody'll come here and throw Magrue out on his ass and that way they won't have to put up with him no more. That'll happen if the professor takes all that Spanish horseshit, or even word of it, back with him. But it ain't that simple. He can't just let the stuff go that easy—or even show it to the professor. On account of it's sacred."

"Sacred?" repeated Professor Ashley, his fine-cut eyebrows forming little raised arches. "What makes you say that?"

"The white man thinks the Indian's got a religion, maybe because that's the only word for it in the white man's language. Well, the Indian thinks about spirits and stuff like that, but it ain't like goin' to church every Sunday. It's more like there was some kind o' magic that crops up everywhere and everyday. It's all tied up with the tribe itself, and it's different with each tribe."

"Fascinating," said the professor. "I've sensed some of that, but I haven't been able to express it as eloquently and knowledgeably as you do, Joe."

Joe ignored the compliment—maybe not sure that was what it was. "Now the Zama," he continued, "they got Pa-yat-ya-ma, the Sun Father, and the Coyote twins with their magic hoops, and the sacred fire that don't never die, and all that stuff—more'n you could ever remember unless you was a Zama yourself, and all that's somethin' like what the other tribes got, though not exactly. What they got that's real special is what they call—how the hell can I translate this?—That-Which-Be-longs-to-the-Golden-Gods."

"What in hell are you talkin' about, Joe?" asked Raider.

"That Spanish stuff the professor's after. You see, when them Spanish soldiers come here hundreds of years ago they didn't treat the Zama like they did some o' the other tribes. The way they tell the old tale, it was some offshoot from Coronado's army that come here—maybe a company or a troop or somethin' like that."

"Led by one Captain Alfonso de Rojas, to be exact," said the professor.

"Yeah—well, this hombre's name don't matter. What counts is that he wasn't like most o' the others and didn't just barge in killin' off all the men and rapin' all the women. In fact, it was one o' them years when everything was dried up and the Zama were starvin', and this here Spanish gent, who had guns, which they never seen before, went out and hunted game and got food for 'em. And he musta been in some kinda trouble with his own kind, 'cause he and his men settled down here and never did go back to their goddamned army."

"That is precisely how the old records have it," exact," said the professor.

"Anyway," Joe continued, "they figured this here captain and his men was gods sent to deliver them. The Golden Gods, they called 'em—still do. And they mixed 'em in with all their other gods, and now they're part of their religion. Which they keep up, secretly from the missionaries, like all the other tribes."

Raider nodded thoughtfully. "I reckon I see this now, Joe. They don't want strangers pokin' around in any of that stuff the Spaniards left, because it's part of their worship."

"Figured you'd get it sooner or later," Joe said, with a touch of sarcasm.

Raider glanced at Joe. "Where do they keep the stuff?"

"They ain't tellin' nobody that," said Joe, "but it's my guess it's in the kiva—or close to it."

"The sacred place," said the professor. "Interesting that it's underground. It expresses a return to the womb of the Earth Mother."

"Well, all this is good to know, I guess," said Raider, "but it still ain't gettin' us any closer to those pots and pans. And I'm beginning to think I'm wastin' my time here. Besides, I'm worried about Doc. He ought to have showed up by now."

"But we can't leave now!" said Genevieve. "Not while there's still a chance we'll see the artifacts!"

Raider shrugged. "You two can stay if you want. I better mosey off and find out what the hell's goin' on out there."

Joe Sunbird spat into the dust again. "Just one thing maybe you ain't thought about, Raider."

"What's that?"

"Like I say, the chief ain't decided yet what he's gonna do. And, like I say, there's a lotta ways he might turn. I expect he's waitin' for a sign to tell him what to do—like seein' the shape of some cloud, or the way a prairie hawk flies by, or somethin' like that. That sign could turn his thinkin' right around in the other direction. He might figure the professor knows too much already, and that nobody else on the outside ought to know it, and that the professor better not get out of here at all."

Genevieve's eyebrows rose. "You mean you think he'd actually try to hold us prisoners?"

Joe looked at her for a long moment, then said, "The Zama don't take prisoners. Never have."

Raider nodded slowly. "Could be Joe's right about that. Like he says, I hadn't figured on it. Just didn't know enough about these here Zama to see it."

"Then what on earth are we going to do?" asked Genevieve, now genuinely alarmed.

"Only one thing *to* do," said Raider, still frowning with thought. "Get out of here slow and easy, before they realize it. If the old chief decides to help the professor out pretty soon, well and good, but I think we better slip away before he hits on somethin' like Joe just said. Anyway, I'm not leavin' you two alone here now."

"Thank you for that, Raider," said Genevieve, her eyes suddenly showing more regard for him than they had exhibited previously.

"Forget it," said Raider, secretly hoping she wouldn't. He might, by golly, get to know that marvelous body of hers yet. That would really give him and Doc something in common. "Now look," he continued. "Here's what we better do. Let's let Joe duck out first. They know him and kinda trust him; they won't stop him from leavin'. What I want you to do, Joe, is head for Santa Fe and see if you can find out what happened to Doc. Tell him where we are, and what's happening, and to get his ass here fast, except he's to come up on the rock real slow and under cover, just in case we've run into trouble by that time. Think you can do that?"

Joe shrugged. "Sure. There's whiskey in Santa Fe. I'll need some *dinero* for it."

"The professor'll fix you up," said Raider. "Won't you, Professor?"

"Eh? What? Yes, of course. Whatever you say, Mr. Raider."

"Get there fast as you can, Joe," said Raider. "No sidetracks on the way."

"Look, I know how to get there," grumbled Joe. "I know this goddamn country like the back o' my hand. Quickest way there ain't a straight line, either, like you might think. You go straight, you hit the Brazos where you can't cross it. Best place to cross is a little north, just below Tesqua."

"I don't care how you go, just get there," said Raider. "You do this right and the professor'll buy you a whole barrel of whiskey."

"A whole barrel?" said Genevieve. "Why, that will cost a fortune!"

"Damn right," said Raider. "And what you're buyin' is maybe your life—so just do like I say."

Genevieve sighed and said, "Very well, Raider."

Raider nodded with satisfaction. Genevieve was looking at him almost submissively now—at any rate, with a new respect. It just might make her more tractable all around. Like, if the time and place fell together right and they found themselves alone. Probably he shouldn't be thinking about something like that at a time like this, but when you looked at Genevieve, with her broad shoulders and swelling bosoms, you just couldn't help thinking along those lines no matter what else was on your mind.

He rose from his hunkered-down position. "Everybody act natural now, like we meant to stay here," he said. "I want to get the lay of the land a little more and figure out how we can slip away. Might even take us a day or two to get to it. Anyway, you two look me up in my room about midnight—I'll have some information for you then about how we're gonna do it. Meantime, just go on about your business like nothin's changed." He surveyed them for a moment to be sure they understood. Then he nodded again. "See y'all later," he said, and wandered off with a languid stride.

She was waiting in the gunpowder house, as she had promised. It was twilight, soft and pinkish gray, when Raider descended the ladder there; she came from the shadows as he stepped down upon the floor, and he took her into his arms. She was breathing hard and trembling. She felt fragile in his embrace, and he was tender with her—maybe a little more so than he sometimes was with other women.

Within moments they had taken off their clothes and were stretched out on the blanket Kara had brought. He was pleased when his eyes became more used to the near-darkness; the sight of her, as slim and compact as she was, delighted him and added another dimension to the pleasure he found in her. He ran his palm over her body, feeling its firm, silken smoothness, tracing out the subtle contours of her breasts with their hard little nipples, then her taut, flat belly, and the nap of the soft and somewhat sparse hair below it. Raider had had a Chinese gal on occasion, and they were real light on the hair there, too, for some reason. Maybe Indians and Chinese were related in some way—the professor would probably know more about that than he did.

Responding to Raider's preliminary play, quivering with desire now, Kara pushed him on his back and, starting at his neck, began to rub the tip of her nose, Indian-fashion, on his skin, lowering herself gradually down the length of his torso until she came to his member, already a rigid column that seemed about to burst from its expansion. Then, cupping his testicles in her hands, she mouthed its prepuce hungrily, rolling her tongue on the sensitive underside until Raider, feeling himself go wonderfully mad, thought he might float up through the trapdoor and keep on rising till he reached the moon.

He stiffened his legs a little to hold himself in, so he'd be able to finish off the regular way when they got around to it, and at that Kara looked up and whispered, "It's all right, Raider. I want you to come. I want to taste you!"

She was on him again, mouthing hotly, her spittle rolling down his cock and becoming cool where it moistened the pubic hair below. Raider let himself go, thrusting spasmodically. She gobbled his sperm hungrily, and he felt her shudder so hard he knew she'd reached her own climax simultaneously.

There was one thing about Raider that made him figure he was lucky. He was in great physical shape, and once he'd shot his wad it didn't take him long to work up a new one. Kara appreciated that, too, and was more than ready for him when he got it up again a short time later, rolled her on her back, and mounted her in conventional fashion. That was good, too, and, as always with the second time, took a little longer. She moaned loudly, all but screaming with the ecstasy he was giving her.

The pauses between their copulations became longer. After a while he was breathing harder; there was a limit somewhere, even for a man like Raider. She lay with her head on his thighs, occasionally darting her tongue forward to lick his semisoft cock playfully.

"I have never had such joy, Raider," she said. "As I told you, I tried it before, now and then. But it was never like this."

"Glad we get along good," said Raider, hoping the conversation wouldn't get too serious.

"I came to the white man's world with my Indian ways—which I still prefer," she said. "And I wondered long about many of the white man's ways. What they called love. The idea that somehow, out of all the people in the world, one man and one woman are meant for each other. I could never understand it, Raider, but now—well, now I think I do."

He frowned a little. "Take it easy, Kara. I've got strong feelin's about you, too, but we mustn't, neither one of us, let 'em go too far. You got the way you're goin', and I've got my way. They just don't point to the same place. To tell you the truth, Kara, I probably don't point right for any woman, anywhere."

"I love you, Raider."

He breathed in and out deeply. "Sweet words, all right—nice to hear—but I wish you wouldn't say 'em."

"I want to do something for you."

"You just did." He smiled dryly.

"That's not what I mean. You *don't* know what it is to love, do you? What it means to a woman. She wants to do more for her man than rut with him like some animal—though that part of it's fine, too. She wants to help him some way—serve him. Perhaps that is my Indian side speaking now."

"Just be your own sweet self, Kara," he said gently, stroking her hair. "That's enough for me."

She brought her head up suddenly, then moved her body until it was parallel with his and she was looking into his eyes—what she could see of them in the darkness. "I will show you That-Which-Belongs-to-the-Golden-Gods," she said abruptly.

"The stuff those Spanish soldiers left?" he said in surprise.

"Yes! Get dressed. Come with me. But we must move quietly and not be seen."

He still didn't understand quite why she wanted to show him the artifacts, though he figured it might have made more sense to him if he knew a little more about the ways of the Indians and especially the ways of Indian women. At any rate, he'd been curious about the damned things for some time now, and this was a good chance to get a look at them. He did as Kara bade him, and presently they climbed out of the little building and crossed the rock table to the village proper, where the kiva protruded like a pillbox from the ground near the central plaza.

The blue-black sky was clear and filled with stars, as usual, and the air, high on the plateau, was as clean as spring water. The desert night was cool on their cheeks. Kara first looked this way and that, and, seeing that no one was in sight, led him quickly to the kiva and to the trapdoor in its turret-like roof.

Once inside, she found a tallow torch on one wall, along with a box of kitchen matches, for the Zama were not above adopting some of the white man's conveniences. When the torch sputtered into flame, Raider saw that they were in a large circular room that had sand paintings on the floor at one end. These had been made with great skill by pouring lines and areas of different colored sands in miniature crevices in the floor, and Raider understood that the symbols depicted had religious significance, though he didn't know precisely in what ways.

"Only the men of the council and Those-Who-

Can-See-the-Spirits are allowed in here," she whispered. "We mustn't be discovered."

"Figured as much," said Raider, nodding wryly.

At the far end of the room was a wattled door that Raider could see was not hinged but merely removed to open the passageway it led to. As they neared it, he saw the torch Kara carried flicker in the draft that came from it, indicating some unseen means of ventilation farther on. Bent in the low passageway, they moved forward for what he judged to be about twenty feet along a slight downward incline, and then emerged into a chamber that he thought of as roughly parlor-sized. Kara stood in the center of it, holding the torch high, and Raider looked at the room in amazement.

It was a small museum. There were chests against the walls, a suit of armor in one corner, swords and lances and even hats hanging on the walls, and scattered among everything were what appeared to be canteens and cooking vessels of the kind soldiers might carry. The most remarkable piece, which lay on the floor by one of the chests, was a small cannon of bronze mounted on a gimbal that looked like a large slingshot; ancient warships had had such cannon, Raider knew, but this looked like a variation designed for a wheeled vehicle, perhaps a wagon.

Kara now opened one of the miniature chests. Necklaces, rings, and medallions were piled in it carelessly. Most were of gold and silver and many were studded with jewels that must have been rubies or emeralds. It was clear that each chest contained a small fortune, and, altogether, there were four of them.

"One o' those'd set a man up for life," said Raider, staring.

She smiled faintly. "I know it must be a temptation, but you can't steal one. You wouldn't get far before they'd hunt you down. Even if you did get away, they'd send assassins after you to the ends of the earth."

"Well, I ain't gonna try," said Raider, and then, with a sigh, added, "but I must admit it crossed my mind." He brought his head up again, abruptly. "Speakin' of gettin' away, that's what we all figure on doin' soon as we can. We got an idea the chief ain't gonna make up his mind for some time, and that maybe even then he might make it up the wrong way."

She stared at him for a moment. "I knew that sometime you would have to leave, Raider."

"You can go with us, if you want. Though don't count on us bein' together afterward."

"No," she said, shaking her head. "My place is here, and I will stay. It will sadden me to see you go, but I will not stand in your way. You're right about us, Raider. We have different paths to follow."

"Well, what I was startin' to say," continued Raider, glancing around the room, "is that there must be some kind of passageway here, the way the air comes through."

She nodded. "Your guess is correct. Come—I will show you."

Moving to a darker corner, she showed him a low opening similar to the one that had led from the kiva to the chamber. She led the way along a low tunnel for a fairly long distance as it followed a gentle curve, and presently they were at an opening high on the side of the rock overlooking the desert floor. It was a long drop to the foot of the rock; Kara pointed downward. "There are footholds cut into the rock so that one can climb down. You would never notice them from below. Not as easy to use as steps, but it can be done. This was built long ago, of course, as a way of escape in case of siege."

"Looks to me like exactly what we need. All we got to do is get down there and circle around to where they got our horses; I took a good look and saw they ain't guarded. I don't expect the chief'll like it much, but if we haven't stole anything he won't follow too hard. And we won't be weighted down, so we can travel fast."

"Even so," said Kara gravely. "It will be dangerous."

"Yup," said Raider, nodding. "Things get that way sometimes."

They turned and retraced their steps back to the chamber with the artifacts, and there Raider took one more long look at the jewelry chests before Kara brought him back again into the kiva. She paused, ready to douse the torch and hang it in its place again. Her eyes, as she sought Raider's eyes, switched back and forth like the tip of a cougar's tail. "We haven't much longer to be together."

"Reckon not," said Raider.

"It is as it must be. But I will always remember you, Raider. I will always remember how, at least once, I knew what it was to be in love."

"Well, I won't be forgettin' you too quick, either," he said seriously.

"Let us go back to the gunpowder room. Our last night. Let us make the most of it."

"Suits me," Raider said. "But I gotta meet the professor and Genevieve first; promised 'em I would to tell 'em how we can get out of here. You wait for me, okay?"

"Don't be long. And kiss me now."

Raider had never thought much about how a man and woman just naturally close their eyes when they're kissing. Folks like the professor, who were always asking questions about everything, might wonder about it, but as far as he was concerned it was the way something was, and since it somehow made kissing even better, there wasn't much point in thinking about it.

When Raider and Kara at last broke apart, and opened their eyes again, they saw immediately that they were not alone in the kiva.

At the bottom of the ladder stood the stocky, white-haired chief, Tabaydeh, flanked by four warriors, two on each side. They held lances, pointed at Raider and Kara. Raider had never heard them enter—or else they'd been here all the time. One of the warriors lowered his lance long enough to light another torch, and, in its flickering light, Raider saw the smoldering anger in the old man's eyes.

"Oh, hell," said Raider, staring back. "Tell him we're sorry."

Kara was trembling, and not with passion this time. "That will not help," she said. "There is no need to say anything. We have violated the kiva. It means only one thing."

"Yeah? What's that?"

She turned to look at him, her large dark eyes molten with despair. "Can't you guess, Raider?"

"Now, hold on here. Are you sayin'—?"

"Look at Tabayadeh, Raider. Closely. Then you will know, as I do, that now he must kill us all."

Raider stared at the chief and tried to let what Kara had said sink into his head. It sank slowly.

CHAPTER THIRTEEN

Doc Weatherbee was already numb, so he didn't feel the chill of the icy water and the cool air in the shadow of the gorge as much as he might have. He felt it some, of course, and his teeth were trying to chatter with it, but his general state was closer to a daze than it was to his usual awareness.

He was crouched in a patch of cattail reeds, downriver from where he'd plunged into the torrent, and he was crouched not only because he wanted concealment but also because he might not have been able to rise even if he wanted to. All the strength seemed to have left his body; all acuity seemed to have gone from his mind. Only dimly now was he remembering what had happened, some of it clear in recollection, other parts of it filled in by assumption and imagination.

Hitting the water must have knocked him out clean, for several seconds anyway. In one moment he was striking the churning river, in the next he was already engulfed by it, tumbling over and over as the current swept him along. He remembered wanting to gasp for breath, then realizing that if he did he'd gasp in water, not air. He remembered that his chest started hurting, the way he was holding his breath, and he remembered clawing desperately at the water to somehow bring his head above it. Just when he thought he'd black out again, the water itself tossed him upward, and, with his head momentarily out of it, he drew in all the air his lungs would take.

After that he was tumbled again, swept from

side to side, and rolled in a series of dizzying somersaults. He wasn't sure how long this went on; it came to him in bits and pieces. And then, suddenly, he felt himself carried into a pool of stiller water formed by a bend, barely missing a sharp boulder as he was thrown past it, and when his hand shot out this time it grasped the stalk of one of the cattails that concealed him now. He didn't remember pulling himself farther into the reeds, but he must have done that, because here he was.

Somewhere deep down, a part of him must have been working on his dilemma, because he didn't consciously recall thinking that concealment might be a good idea. But now that his mind was clearing a bit, he saw that it was, for the odds were damned good that Magrue and his two men would be coming down here to make sure he'd drowned—or maybe even because they'd seen him go into the cattails and knew he hadn't, though Doc had an idea the reed patch was far enough downriver to be out of their sight.

It was still hard for him to measure time in his head, so he wasn't sure how long he'd been crouching before he heard voices. Trying to ignore the aching all through his body, he came alert and turned his eyes toward them, though for the moment he couldn't see anything.

"Goddamn, but the river's fast!" said Magrue's voice. "Looked like hardly anything up where we were. Hell, he's probably miles away by now."

"Then why're we still lookin'?" said Busby's voice.

"To do it right, that's why. To check and make sure. To keep from fouling everything up, the way you did with those ropes—and Cristóbal did with that nag. What's the point of my making a plan when you two can't carry it out?"

"Hell's bells, Seth, don't get your bowels all in an uproar," said Busby. "Everything worked out like you wanted. Weatherbee can't be alive—no man could after a fall like that. They'll find his body downriver somewheres, mark my words. And we *did* finally manage to push that stupid broomtail over, so they'll find its carcass, too, and it'll all be just like you figured it would. Poor Doc Weatherbee. Slipped and went over. Too bad, but it could happen to anybody."

The voices had stopped moving along now; evidently the men had paused not too far from where Doc was hiding. "Well, chances are it's that way," said Magrue's voice, louder than the others, as though he were performing on a stage and wanted to be heard in the back of the hall. "But I'd feel a lot better if I saw Doc's body and could be a hundred percent sure."

"You worry too much," grunted the sheriff. "We didn't even have to take that long climb down here. Goin' to be a sonofabitch gettin' up again."

"It'll do you good," said Magrue. "It'll take some of that lard off you. Don't think you're going to get a good rest, either, as soon as we get back. There's still plenty to do."

"Like what?" Busby was clearly not in love with the prospect of any vigorous activity.

"You know damn well what," said Magrue. "We've got to put a small army together here. At least twenty men—and they've got to be ones we can trust, and ones who can handle firearms. Try to get veterans, if you can. Some'll already be on hand, but you'll just have to dig up the others, ride out to their spreads or wherever they are to get 'em. And don't look so put-upon, Harold—I'll be doing the same thing."

"How come you need so many, anyway?"

"Christ, you don't foresee anything, do you? Those Indians on Spanish Rock aren't going to just let us come up there with the red carpet rolled out and the band playing 'Dixie.' And that rock'd be hard to take with two old ladies and a pointy-headed idiot defending it. It's going to have to be a siege. Till we wear 'em down enough to make the assault."

After a moment's pause, Busby said, "Gonna take time to get everybody together."

"I know that. That's why I want you to get off your ass and move fast. So let's stop wasting time, and get to it!"

Doc heard their scuffling footsteps recede in the direction they'd come from, and presently there was no sound but the harsh purring of the water beyond the rocks. With some of his strength returning now, he lifted his head experimentally, peered over the cattails, and saw that no one was in sight. Swinging his gaze to the left, he detected the three men in the distance, where they'd already crossed the river over some boulders that formed a series of stepping stones. They were beginning their climb out of the gorge at a place where the slope was still steep but at least not vertical.

Waiting for them to reach the top and then move out of sight wasn't easy, for Doc wanted to get going, but he forced patience on himself. When at last they were out of sight, he rose fully, wobbled a little as he stood there, then stumbled through the shallow water to the shore.

Make a list of any man's most basic necessities, and Doc at the moment had none of them. He could have used rest, food, relief from pain, and even a woman to stroke him some—not necessarily in that order. He staggered as he pushed on, and he kept falling. There was another, less-steep slope on the western face of the gorge—a worn trail seemed to indicate that this was a favored crossing place—and Doc started up this sharp incline, clawing his way, pausing every few steps to catch his breath and let all his throbbing pains subside a little. The desert floor was up there—maybe another sixty or seventy feet. If you reached it and headed west you'd get to Spanish Rock. At the pace he could make afoot he'd reach it by A.D. 1900 or thereabouts. But he had to try. Had to warn Raider that Magrue was coming with, as he'd called it himself, a small army. Had to find out if that sonofabitch partner of his had made it yet to the sweet moss between Genevieve's thighs.

Not necessarily in that order.

Christ, he was thinking crazy now—losing his mind.

He was at the top. Seemed to be, anyway. The shimmering heat waves from all the desert that stretched away from him started to rock and spin. The whole world turned over, with the sun and the horizon and everything else in the wrong place. Goddamn it, was he going to black out again? Nothing but crazy, swimming colors in front of his eyes. Getting gray . . . darkening. He was pitching forward, falling—

He was face down on the ground. He didn't remember hitting it. Somebody was shaking his shoulder.

"Go the hell away," Doc muttered wearily.

"Hey, Doc!" said a familiar voice. "What the hell you think you're doin' here?"

Either he rolled over under his own power or the person who'd shaken his shoulder rolled him. Hard to say which. Doc blinked, things sharpened a bit once more in his eyes, and he looked up to see the face of Joe Sunbird, with all its sun-weathered striations and that stupid-looking black patch over one eye.

"Glad to see you," said Doc. "Never thought I would be."

"Thought you was in Santa Fe. Goin' there to find you."

"Well, I'm not. Joe, listen. Got to get to Spanish Rock. Tell Raider who's comin'."

"What?"

"Don't ask a lot of fool questions. You got a horse?"

"Two." Joe nodded toward them. "One's supposed to be for you."

"Then help me on it, goddamn it," said Doc, "and let's get goin'. I'll explain everything on the way."

CHAPTER FOURTEEN

Atop Spanish Rock, and in the village near the central plaza, was a sheep corral much like the one in the valley below where the sheep were brought from the hills to be sheared. Raider wasn't sure why it was here—perhaps as a slaughter pen, he thought, for the few sheep that became part of the food supply—but the Zama had now made use of it as a holding pen for their new prisoners. He, the professor, Genevieve, and Kara were in this fenced area as dawn broke, herded together as though *they* were sheep, and, as far as the slaughter part of it was concerned, that was just about what they were.

They had been bound firmly to one of the rails, placed there four abreast. Guards, who were armed with lances and an assortment of ancient rifles, and who kept constant eyes upon them, were ringed around the corral. Beyond the guards, they could see the preparations that had been going on all night, by torchlight at first, and now in the slowly brightening, peach-colored glow of the dawn.

Along with the others, Professor Ashley was watching a group of women sweep the plaza, while a group of men finished tamping the loose dirt around a sturdy ten-foot pole that had been set into the ground. "It's occurred to me," he said mildly, "that not many outsiders have been able to watch this sort of thing. Fascinating."

"Father!" said Genevieve sternly. "Can't you get it into your head what's happening?"

"Well, yes, I suppose I can," said the professor,

sighing. "We are in a bit of danger, aren't we? I must confess, however, I find it hard to believe it's real. It's just too overwhelming for that, I suppose."

"It's real, all right," grunted Raider. "Better be thinkin' how to deal with it, not how fascinating it is."

"How to deal with it?" Genevieve looked at him sharply. "Do you have an idea?"

"Not one damn idea, at the moment," said Raider, frowning.

"There *must* be some hope," said Genevieve, her usually cool and self-possessed voice becoming a touch shaky. "Perhaps they just mean to frighten us—teach us a lesson or something like that—then send us on our way."

Kara shook her head. "It's not a bluff. The law of the kiva has been violated. Tabaydeh is required to arrange punishment."

"That still doesn't make sense, Kara," Genevieve said stubbornly. "First, apparently you and Raider violated the kiva, not Father and I. Second, how can he simply decide we're all guilty—just like that—without some sort of trial?"

"You must realize that you are no longer back in your own world, Miss Ashley," Kara said. "What Tabaydeh decides doesn't come from books, where it's all written down in black and white, but from what the spirits tell him. He has eaten the peyote; he has listened to the drum; he has seen the colors on the walls. I am of Zama blood, too, and I know how he thinks. It is more nearly correct to say that he *feels,* rather than thinks."

"But can't he see he's making a big mistake? If we don't return, questions will be asked. They might even send a troop of soldiers out to look for us!"

Kara shook her head. "You know as well as I do

that that's doubtful. We have a saying: 'You can paint the skin of a cougar, but you cannot paint his bones.' Tabaydeh seemed friendly to you when you first came here, and, as a matter of fact, he at first wished you no harm. He didn't show it, but he was even then as wary as a cougar inside. The spirits had done something curious, something puzzling, in sending strangers who knew about what the Golden Gods had left here. For all he knew, there was some reason for it—perhaps if the strangers took some of the artifacts attention would be drawn to the way Magrue was treating the Zama and all the other tribes. So he delayed in deciding what to do, waiting for the spirits to tell him more. He had already decided to send you away empty-handed when he found us in the kiva—he was looking for me so that I could tell you this. When he found me with Raider, it was another sign. It told him that none of you could be allowed to return. I have already spoken with Tabaydeh, and I know that this is what's in his mind."

"Mighty fancy," said Raider, scowling, his eyes still darting here and there in the plaza as he took in all the preparations. "But it don't seem to do us a hell of a lot of good, the way things stand."

"But," insisted Genevieve, "he hasn't even talked to us. He's made no attempt to hear our side of the story. That's not fair!"

"If you are innocent," said Kara, "the spirits will make that clear."

"How?"

Kara nodded toward the men who were testing the firmness of the upright pole. "After the dance, we will be taken there one by one. The archers will send arrows at us, across the plaza. Three arrows each. If all three arrows miss, that person is innocent and will be set free."

"Interesting," said the professor. "The ordeal, rather than the trial. It is common in primitive societies."

"For God's sake, Father!" cried Genevieve.

"Uh, sorry," muttered Ashley, scowling with embarrassment.

Genevieve looked at Raider again. "There *is* a chance, then. If those arrows miss—"

"Don't count on it," growled Raider. He continued to watch the preparations.

As the sun rose blazing into the morning sky, the Indians formed lines, standing abreast, each line facing the other across the plaza, and then the drums began to sound, and they started their dance, shuffling lightly at first, increasing the intensity of their movements as the hollow drumbeats began to stir them.

They were dressed in their finest for the ceremonial occasion. Women and men wore all of their silver and turquoise jewelry, and their brightest garments. In with the dancers were the men of the secret societies, the Coyote, the Red-tailed Hawk, the Rattlesnake, and the Cougar, dressed in the skins and feathers of each symbolic animal. Tabaydeh, the chief, was in plainer dress, along with his principal advisors, who surrounded him as he stood quietly in place at the far end of the plaza. His long white hair, gleaming in the sun and stirring in the faint breeze, was its own ceremonial headdress.

The chanting began, low at first, rising in pitch as the sun climbed.

Four archers, each with a quiver of three arrows, moved into place near the chief and stood there at stiff attention.

"I'm sorry," Kara said in a soft voice, primarily

to Raider, but loud enough for the others to hear, too. "It is all my fault. If I had not taken Raider to the kiva this would not have happened. Well, I'll die for that, which is as it should be. But I'm sorry that all of you have to die, too."

"This is a fine time to realize it," said Genevieve primly.

"Forget it," Raider said curtly. "Lookin' for blame don't get us anywhere."

Genevieve glared at him. "Doc was right about you, Raider. You're callous and selfish. You're— you're a savage, just as these Indians are!"

"Shut up," said Raider. "I'm tryin' to think."

Moments later Raider was surprised to hear Kara, beside him, murmuring softly, and when he looked at her he saw that she had closed her eyes and was beginning to chant with the others. Her feet were starting to move in the shuffling step of the dance. Something in her blood—something burning and primitive, something that had always been there—was eroding away the thin crust of civilization she'd acquired in all her years of schooling.

As for Raider, he *was* trying to think, just as he'd told Genevieve. Common sense told him the odds were overwhelmingly against his actually thinking of anything to get them out of this, but grabbing for it in your mind, which was something like grabbing at empty air in the dark, kept you too busy to stew over what was going to happen, and that way you bore the brunt of it only once, when it actually happened.

The drumming and the chanting stopped abruptly. Becoming alert, Raider saw the chief gesture, saw the lines of dancers shuffle back into their original place, and saw the warriors of Tabaydeh's special guard trot toward the corral. Each of these

men carried a percussion musket of huge caliber
—old Jake Hawken guns from the fur-trapping
days of the 1840s, they looked like—and it was
Raider's guess that these primitive pieces were
about the best the Indians had. They were as ceremonial as the feathered lances and the head-
dresses; when it came to serious business, their
bows and arrows were much more effective as
weapons.

The guardsmen entered the corral and, without
further delay, marched up to Genevieve, one stepping forward to loosen her bonds.

"Damn all of you!" Genevieve cried at them bitterly. "You can't do this! You just *can't!*"

Raider sighed. At least she was bucking them,
right to the last, instead of folding up in terror and
despair, and that much of her he had to admire.
He'd feel bad, real bad, about her when she was
gone, and he had no doubt that Doc, if he ever
learned what had happened, would feel even worse.

The warriors walked her roughly to the post and
bound her there, facing the chief and the archers,
who were across the plaza, perhaps fifty yards distant. Raider noticed that when they bound her the
rope came tight around her torso, just below her
breasts, so that they seemed to swell out even more
than before, and, in some odd way, there was defi-
ance in the way her upturned chin and those magnificent breasts pointed themselves toward her
captors.

"God keep your soul, Genevieve," murmured the
professor, staring. "And God forgive me for bringing you here."

Kara, who had ceased chanting as the others did,
stared impassively.

The men who had brought Genevieve to the post
withdrew. Tabaydeh gestured at the first archer,

who stepped forward, fitting an arrow to his bow. A solitary drum began to sound in slow rhythm, at about the pace of a heartbeat.

Tabaydeh spoke a soft word Raider couldn't hear.

The archer raised his bow and took aim.

Crazy dreams were going through Doc Weatherbee's head, and he knew only in intermittent flashes that he lay in a shaded spot on the ground —under the bank of a deeply cut arroyo, if he wasn't mistaken—with Joe Sunbird kneeling beside him wiping his brow with a moist rag that was relatively cool. He wasn't sure how long this had been going on; he didn't exactly remember halting and being stretched out here, which was what Joe must have done for him.

There was an interval now when his wits had returned to him. "Goddamn it, Joe, what am I doin' here?"

"You take it easy, Doc. Fell off your horse. You ain't in no shape to ride."

"*Gotta* ride." Doc struggled to raise himself and couldn't. "Gotta tell Raider Magrue's comin'."

"Don't care if you gotta. You just plumb can't, *primo*. You keep still and maybe pretty soon you can."

"Nothin' wrong with me," said Doc stubbornly. "Little touch of sun, that's all."

"Sure. A touch of sun. But in the shape you're in, that ain't little. It's plenty."

"But we're wastin' time. Look, *you* go warn Raider. Leave me here."

"Leave you here, hey?" Joe Sunbird's one good eye crinkled thoughtfully at Doc. "You know what's gonna happen, you dumb gringo, I leave you here? Buzzards gonna eat you alive. They won't even wait till you're all dead—I seen 'em do that before. If it ain't buzzards, then the first goddamn coyote comes along."

"You leave that to me," said Doc. "No goddamn buzzard's gonna get me, dead *or* alive. I'm too goddamn ornery for 'em."

"You lost your head, gringo. You don' know what you're sayin'."

"The hell I don't! You get your goddamn half-breed ass to Spanish Rock—that's an order!"

"Don't take orders from you," said Joe, shrugging. "Hey, how come you so loco, anyway? You aint' thankin' me, I save your goddamn life, but all you doin' is callin' me names. Why the fuck you can't be nice and polite, like somebody supposed to?"

"Because I can't get through that thick head of yours any other way," retorted Doc.

"Thick head, huh? Well, you listen to me, Señor Quack. Ain't gonna do a goddamn thing, I ride to Spanish Rock. Magrue, he is already there by now."

"What makes you so sure of that?"

" 'Cause he passed us already. Long time ago. With maybe twenty riders, maybe more. Didn't see us here in the arroyo; too far off."

"My God, have I been out that long?" Doc paled. "Even so, we gotta try it. Maybe they got delayed —maybe we can overtake 'em. Put me on that goddamn horse, Joe! Tie me on it if you have to."

He used every ounce of strength that was left to him in one last, desperate effort to rise; he got about halfway up and dizziness overcame him, everything turning pink and rocking crazily before his eyes. When he fell back again, blackness once more descended upon him.

*   *   *

Raider expected the twang of a bowstring, and had braced himself for the sickening sight of an arrow striking Genevieve, to kill her not instantly and mercifully but with lingering pain.

Instead he heard the sound of a shot.

With everyone else, he snapped his head in the direction of that sound—it had come from the head of the stone steps at the eastern edge of the rock plateau. Immediately, he knew what had happened. The sentinel there had discharged his old rifle—it looked, unbelievably, like a flintlock—and was now rushing toward the chief, waving it. Beyond the edge of the rock, in the distance and on the desert floor below, Raider could see a thin cloud of dust pluming away in the light wind. It'd be a lot of riders to make a dust cloud that sizable.

Men were crowding around the old chief and the sentinel now; there was a great deal of gesturing and considerable palaver, which Raider couldn't make out at this distance. Tabaydeh and several of his lieutenants scurried to the edge of the rock and stood there for a moment, peering at the approaching dust cloud. The way they looked at it—intently, murmuring to each other all the while—Raider could believe Joe Sunbird's assertion that the Zama had the eyes of eagles.

Abruptly, the white-haired chief turned from the rim and began to call out what must have been orders, gesturing at various men and various places. Indians scurried here and there, some gathering up firearms they'd momentarily laid aside. The archers who had been about to take part in the execution ran toward the edge of the rock, other archers joining them.

"What's happened?" asked Professor Ashley, with his usual air of mild bewilderment.

"Somebody comin'," said Raider. "The way

they're gettin' ready, it's somebody who ain't exactly welcome. Wouldn't be surprised if it was Magrue."

Raider saw several warriors release Genevieve from the post where she'd been bound and then bring her back to the corral. By this time the chief himself was approaching his captives. He spoke rapidly to Kara.

"That is Magrue out there," she translated. "With many men, many guns. It's clear he knows of the treasure in the kiva. He means to attack; he has never come here before in such numbers and so heavily armed."

"How in hell did he find out?" Raider asked. "Damned if I ever told him. And I didn't even know for sure till I saw the stuff."

"Tabaydeh says you're to be put inside," she continued. "We must do what we can now to keep Magrue from storming the rock."

"And what about you? Are you still a prisoner?"

"Of course. The, uh—" She looked around the plaza, now filled with scurrying warriors. "The ceremony is not cancelled. It is merely postponed."

Raider sighed deeply. "Well, that's better'n nothin'. But while I got the chance, I got somethin' to say to the chief."

"Say it quickly, then."

"If he's smart, he'll forget about killin' us off and let us help him keep Magrue from gettin' here. That means me, mainly, but the pardon includes Genevieve and the professor. And you, too, Kara. Tell him that, and tell him he can use me in this little battle he's about to have on his hands. The Zama may have eyes like eagles, but I can still shoot straighter'n any of 'em—I think the chief knows that."

He waited while she relayed this to Tabaydeh.

The old man seemed to retreat into his myriad wrinkles for a moment as he thought it over. His eyes met Raider's; they took on a misty look as though distant campfires burned in them. He finally uttered a brief phrase.

"He will wait for a sign," Kara said.

"Might be too late by the time he gets one," said Raider.

"There is no use trying to persuade him," Kara said. "He will wait."

At the chief's bidding, warriors untied Raider and Ashley from the corral fence, then led them toward the ladder against the high wall of one of the buildings overlooking the plaza.

CHAPTER FIFTEEN

The return of Doc's strength, and, along with it, his clarity of mind, came as slowly as the passage of the fat and waxen moon across the sky. There was no one moment when he realized he was himself again—almost himself, at any rate—but there was a time, somewhere in the darkness of the morning just before dawn, when he could raise his head, blink, look around and take stock, and see at last where he was, where he was going, and how he was getting there.

Astride two nondescript horses, he and Joe Sunbird were riding westward over the low, rolling hills of the desert. In the shimmering moonlight they were like ocean swells. Somehow, Doc knew now, Joe had put him on a horse; somehow he had stayed there, and now that he was coming out of his feverish daze he was able to grip the saddle with his thighs and keep his balance without conscious effort.

The horses were walking. Doc would have preferred them to be at a gallop, but he knew they wouldn't last very long that way. It was only in the dime novels of Ned Buntline and other popular writers of the western scene that horses chased pell-mell for sixty miles without even getting lathered.

He looked at Joe, lean and scrawny, riding in a loose slouch, his unpatched eye looking dead ahead.

"Joe—"

"Yeah?"

"What the hell came over me back there?"

"Goddamn, *you* supposed to know. You supposed to be the doctor."

"I'm a vet, Joe. And the 'Doc' is kinda honorary. All I know is after you picked me up I just kept comin' and goin'."

Joe shrugged. "You got cold in the water. Then hot in the sun. Too much o' that can drop a man."

"I guess that's it." Doc sighed and nodded. "I expect Magrue thinks I'm dead, and I damn near made him right about it. Anyway, he's got a surprise comin' when we get there. If it ain't too late."

The half-breed turned slowly to look at him for a moment. "What the hell we gonna do when we get there? Two of us—all them men Magrue's got."

"Don't know yet. Not exactly. Kinda depends on what the situation is. Magrue's gonna have to storm that rock to get to the treasure he's after. If there *is* a goddamn treasure. And he ain't gonna do that too quick. Like Chickamauga all over again."

"Like what?"

"Civil War battle. In Tennessee. Ended up with Bragg and his Confederates holdin' Missionary Ridge, and General Thomas and General Sheridan chargin' up the slope to take it. Shouldn't have worked, but it did."

"Never heard of it." Joe spat off the horse's near side and into the dust. "You hombres back east was crazy to have that war."

"That's what a lot of people said afterward," said Doc. "Guess they always do, after a war. The time comes when you gotta fight, though. Like with Magrue. He's gone on long enough, takin' over everything, and now he's gotta be stopped."

"Don't see why you and Raider have to stop him. What he does ain't no skin off *your* asses."

"Well," said Doc, "we got a lotta reasons you

don't know about—just take my word for it. And as long as you bring up the subject, how come *you're* pitchin' in against Magrue?"

"Goddamn if I know," said Joe Sunbird, scowling. "Maybe the way he treats the Indians. That bothers half o' me, anyway."

They rode on, and sometime later dawn broke over the desert, sending long shadows ahead of them. It was the best time of day, with the air still cool from the night. With the horses in fair shape, they urged them into a jog. That was when they heard the sound of sporadic gunfire ahead. At that, they put the horses into a full gallop.

At the top of a long, low ridge, they dismounted and, leading the horses, moved forward carefully. Spanish Rock was in sight now, rising from the desert floor like a squat cathedral spire in the distance. They honed their gazes as they stared, and presently they could make out Magrue's riders staked out in a kind of semicircle around the eastern face of the rock, where the steps that led to the top had been carved. The attackers had found concealment behind rocks and in gullies, and they were directing occasional shots toward the rim of the rock whenever they saw, or thought they saw, movement up there. Behind the semicircle, out of range of any rifleshot from the rock, stood several packhorses, tended by one of the attackers who had a campfire going, so that light blue smoke rose thinly into the air and dispersed itself in the almost imperceptible breeze of the morning.

Taking all of this in, Doc nodded. "Looks like Magrue's got the good sense not to charge up the rock right away. See that campfire? That's for three meals a day. Which means he expects to be here a spell. Which means he's gonna starve 'em out or, more likely, let 'em get good and dry. They don't have much of a water supply up there on the rock, I expect, and haul what they need up from the valley. The other thing they'll probably run out of is ammunition. Magrue's been in contact with 'em, like all the pueblos, and he'd know all this."

"Okay," said Joe. "So what good does it do *us* to know it?"

"Don't ask fool questions," said Doc. "I'm tryin' to think."

By standing on tiptoe, Raider was able to watch what was going on outside through a small, high window in the room where he found himself confined with Genevieve. Kara and the professor had been put in an adjacent room, both compartments entered by trapdoors in the roof; there was a thick adobe wall between them and there was no way they could communicate with each other. Raider doubted the Indians had had any particular reason for this arrangement and, escorting the prisoners to the houses, had simply put them where they seemed to fit. And since he'd been thrown in with Genevieve, he didn't mind. Better to be with either her or Kara than with the professor, who, if he was able to see what was happening outside, was probably still making professorial observations about the quaint customs of the Zama tribe.

"It sounds a bit quieter now," said Genevieve, behind him.

He lowered himself and turned from the window. "Yes, and I think I know why."

"Is Magrue giving up?"

He shook his head firmly. "Wish that were it. I've been watching 'em run around out there like bees in a hive. Plenty busy but not gettin' much done. Indians duckin into places and runnin' out again with musket balls and God knows what else.

Truth is, they're runnin' out of ammunition. Plenty of powder, seems like, but just not enough lead to put in those old rifles they got. Some of 'em look left over from Daniel Boone. Anyway, they're savin' their shots, and that's why it's quiet now."

"Do you suppose Magrue realizes this?"

"He'll be guessin' it pretty soon, if he ain't guessed it already. I reckon he's been waitin' for it to happen. He's bound to know the Zama don't have the latest and the best when it comes to firearms."

Genevieve frowned. "That's, uh, that's not very encouraging, is it?"

"It ain't good," Raider agreed, matching her frown. "Soon as Magrue figures they got nothin' more to shoot at him, he's gonna come chargin' up the rock."

"What about their arrows?"

"Well, they got a few left, but they won't last long, either. You don't make arrows by the bucketful, the way you do musket balls. 'Sides, not all of 'em know how to use a bow and arrow. Like a lot of their old ways, it's kinda dyin' out."

Genevieve shuddered. "Raider, what are we going to *do*?"

"Wish I could say somethin' to make you feel better," he said, "but you might as well know the truth. It's my guess Magrue has a good chance of gettin' up here and takin' over."

"Perhaps we're still better off than we were. At least we won't be lined up to be executed, as those Indians were about to do."

He stared at her gravely for a moment. "Jenny," he said, "put yourself in Magrue's place. He can control the Indians later, same as he always has. He might have to kill off a few just to show 'em who's boss, but he don't have to have himself a massacre like them soldiers did at the Washita a few years back, before Custer got his hair lifted at Little Big Horn. The Indians are his excuse for havin' the agency in Tesqua; they're the goose that lays his golden egg. But when it comes to us—you, me, your father—well, it's a little different."

"He wouldn't dare harm us, would he? Too many people would wonder about it."

"Jenny, we know what he's up to—stealin' from the Indians, comin' here after that treasure, and steppin' way out of bounds to do it. He can't afford to let us get outa here alive and go somewhere with what we know. He's *got* to kill us off—he don't have any other choice."

Genevieve stood as though frozen as she returned Raider's stare. He could see that although she believed all he said, she was trying not to; it was just too much to handle. He had to hand her this much: She didn't come apart at the seams with it, the way some gals might have done.

He came forward and gently took her into his arms. She bent her head to his shoulder, reaching it easily, as tall as she was, and then with her pale golden hair against his saddle-tan cheek, she began to weep softly, shivering in his arms.

He let her go on that way for a while.

She lifted her head. She shook it a little, as though to throw off the tears that had moistened her eyes. There was even a slight spreading and relaxing of her lips that was almost a smile. "I hadn't thought about dying out here, Raider. It's hard to get ready for it."

"I don't reckon anybody's ever ready," he said, nodding.

She was examining his lean, hard face as though seeing it for the first time. "Raider—"

"Yeah?"

"Once more before I die."

"Once more what?"

"You know what I mean."

There was a second or two of silence before he understood and nodded again. She backed away from him a step and calmly and deliberately unbuttoned her shirtwaist. Her huge breasts were held in place by a cupped, wraparound device that had lacy edges and looked French to Raider; at any rate it wasn't the corset one might expect, and it looked a lot easier to wear. She reached around in back to unfasten this, and when she removed it those breasts of hers were swelling out toward him in all their pink-capped glory. The rest of her clothes followed swiftly as Raider hastily got rid of his own duds.

Stepping forward again, she clamped herself to his muscled body and pressed hard against him, the breasts crushing down between them as their great nipples hardened. She reached down behind him, hooked her fingers into the curves of his tight rump and pulled his pelvis against hers as hard as she could. She gyrated then, massaging his upright cock between their bellies.

Presently, she slid downward slowly, still clasping him, putting a burning trail of kisses down the center of his torso. He held her head against him. When she was on her knees she engulfed his dong, as long and thick as a warclub, with her lips, and, taking it deep, worked her mouth and tongue upon it, making soft sounds of joy.

In a moment they had both lowered themselves to the floor, and, holding him tightly, she was writhing and rolling back and forth, gasping with pleasure.

"Bring yourself up a little," she whispered. "Straddle me right here—that's it." He was on his knees, his legs spread so that her upper body lay between them. She put his cock into the crack between her mammoth, resilient breasts, and, holding them tightly on each side to grasp his long cylinder firmly, she let him thrust back and forth in the billowing, soft-skinned warmth between them. She brought her head forward a little and, with a flickering tongue, licked the tip of it each time it came near. Raider was tingling all over, holding himself in so he wouldn't explode too soon, going at it just a touch slowly to make it last. He could see where Doc hadn't wanted to share this with him; it was the kind of thing any man would want all for himself, and forever, too—at least while it was going on.

"Now I'll show you how I like to finish," murmured Genevieve. As she had with Doc, she put herself on her hands and knees and presented her exquisitely rounded rump to him. With her thighs slightly spread, he could see the faint shape of her labia and the moist, golden hair that surrounded them deep in the semidarkness of the crevice between her legs. He mounted and reached around to curl his palms over the great, hanging forms of her breasts. He plunged his member forward, into the crevice, and the end of it found the soft opening of her quim and went inside, slanted upward at just the right angle. He kept on thrusting as it sank deeper and deeper into her.

With secret and maybe even a little foolish pride, Raider liked to tell himself he never got exhausted with a woman. He wasn't exhausted now, but he had to admit he was damned near beat. Genevieve was something you'd cross a thousand miles of prairie for and climb over a mountain ridge at the end of it to boot. She was all woman, and there was a hell of a lot more of it packed into her statuesque body than there was with most women. Maybe someday he and Doc would compare notes on her, but he doubted that for two reasons. First, what they did with the women they had wasn't their usual topic of conversation; just the fact that they'd scored—or hadn't—was enough, and they didn't need to trade details. Second, it was likely he wouldn't be around to say *anything* to Doc, wherever the bastard was now, and wherever he'd be once Magrue had finished with Raider.

He was at the window once more, watching the progress of the battle outside. There was no shooting at all now from the top of the rock, and the only sound of gunfire came from occasional distant reports originating in the valley below. At the rim of the rock, near the head of the steps, a squad of eight archers stood at intervals, some rising swiftly now and then to send an arrow downward, then immediately ducking out of sight. Because of the shorter range of the arrows, it was Raider's guess that Magrue and his men were a lot closer now—maybe even beginning their climb up the steps.

A shot sounded from somewhere below, and an archer who had been about to loose a shaft cried out and fell backward, kicking in the dust as he died.

"Goddamn it!" Raider called, though he doubted anyone could hear him. "Let us outa here, you dumb, damn Indians!" He really didn't think they were either dumb or damned; it just seemed the way to put it, under the circumstances.

To his surprise, a voice called back to him from his right side. "Raider! Is that you?"

"Kara?" He turned his head toward her, know-

ing that she was at another window some distance
from the one he was using.

"Can you see everything out there?"

"Hell, yes. How about you?"

"We're watching, too—the professor and I. It—
it doesn't look very good, does it?"

"I reckon you could say that about it," Raider
answered dryly. "Look, isn't there some way we can
all get out? Some way to open them damned trapdoors up above?"

"They're barred from the outside. With heavy
beams. And there's a guard up there, too."

"How do you know there is?"

"I called to him a while ago. He wouldn't answer, though; just growled back for me to be silent."

Raider pressed his forehead down in deepest
thought for a moment. Then he said, "Listen, Kara.
Tell that damned guard to bring the chief here. I
want to talk to him."

"He won't do that. He won't listen."

"Try, Kara. Like you never tried before. Tell him
I'm the only one who knows how we might keep
Magrue from gettin' up here."

"How?"

"Never mind how. Just take my word for it.
Come on, Kara, talk that dumb guard into it. Some
way. You can do it!"

"Wait," she said. "I'll see what I can do."

By putting his ear to the wall, Raider could
faintly hear Kara calling to the guard above,
though he couldn't make out any words—which he
wouldn't have understood in any event.

Genevieve said, "Do you really have some idea?"

"Shut up, Jenny," he said, though gently, as
though chiding a small child.

Kara's voice came from the window again. "Raider?"

"Yeah? What is it?" He was back at the window.

"He'll do it! He's getting the chief now!"

"Good gal," Raider said. "Knew you could!"

Agonizing seconds passed as Raider, watching from the window, saw the guard scuttle, waggling his low ass and short legs across the plaza, like a badger heading for its hole, until he reached Tabaydeh near the head of the steps up the rock. He saw the two men in animated discussion; saw the old chief glance toward his window several times. While this was going on, sporadic shots kept sounding from the valley below, and the archers continued to shoot their dwindling supply of arrows toward the invaders.

Abruptly, the old chief, carrying the ancient percussion rifle for which he had no ammunition, ran toward the structure that housed the prisoners. He stood near the base of the wall and looked up, obviously able to see both Kara and Raider in their windows. He spoke rapidly, and Kara translated.

"What is it? What is this idea you say you have?"

"If it works we go free, okay? No damn drums and dancing; no damn arrows."

"Of course! Speak! Quickly!"

"Let us outa here, chief, and I'll show you what to do."

"You speak first. I am not a fool," he said, Kara translating.

"That there's open to question, chief. No, wait, Kara, don't say that. It'll only get him riled up. Look, tell him he's gonna need me out there, so he might as well let us out right now. Tell him I'm gonna show him how to get some bullets—if we can call 'em that—that'll blast Magrue all to hell."

He waited, tense, as Kara communicated this much to the chief. He met the old man's dark, smoky eyes as they stared up at him for a long moment. Raider didn't know what he put into his own eyes—if it was what he was feeling it was a mixture of impatience and anger—but, whatever it was, the chief seemed to find it suitable. He grunted what must have been an order. Seconds later, the trapdoor in the ceiling opened and a ladder was lowered into the room.

Doc and Joe Sunbird were crawling on their bellies. They had left their horses on the other side of the rise, out of sight, and they were making their way across the hard-baked desert floor, trying to stay in the cover of the twisted chamiso clumps that dotted it. Still in the distance, and at the foot of the great rock, in purple shadow now that the sun was lowering, were Magrue's men in their scattered semicircle, sending shots upward whenever one of the Indian defenders, or any part of one of them, appeared for a moment. Since Doc and Joe had first come upon the scene, the semicircle had tightened. Occasionally, they could see Magrue himself, unmistakable in his buckskin jacket with all its beads and fringes, showing himself long enough to gesture or call out, directing his men ever nearer to the base of the cliff, where the switchback steps that wound up to the summit began.

Between the besiegers and the two crawling men were the packhorses and the campfire, still tended by an hombre who hung back, his eyes intent on the battle in progress. It was a good tactic to keep a resting place with ready chow beyond the perimeter, Doc reflected; Magrue must have had some military training along the line, possibly in the late, great unpleasantness between the states, on one side or the other. And if Doc could ever get his hands on the bastard, he didn't care which side; he'd still mash him to a pulp. Though, considering Magrue's size and beef, that might not turn out to be too easy.

As Joe and Doc snaked forward now, careful to move only when the man at the campfire had his back turned, their tracks came together momentarily and both paused, breathing deeply, at the sinewy roots of a chamiso.

Joe looked at Doc with his one good eye. "What the hell we doin' this for?" he whispered.

"I told you, stupid. To get that man's gun. I don't know exactly what we'll do then, but whatever it is we'll need a gun to do it."

"It won't work. You crazy, Doc."

"Well, you're doin' it with me, aren't you?"

"Yeah. You so damned crazy, I'm gettin' a little crazy, too."

"Hush up, Joe. And keep movin'."

"Shit!" said Joe. But he began to crawl forward again.

As they moved forward now, wriggling their way at intervals, keeping their rumps down, Doc saw Joe, just ahead of him, reach back to his belt, take his hunting knife from its sheath, and put it into his mouth, where it would be handy. They were much nearer the campfire now, and, beyond Joe, Doc could see the man who was guarding it more clearly. He had not payed much attention to him before, but now he saw something familiar in his squat form and rounded, almost humpbacked shoulders. The man turned their way, and they both froze into stillness. He seemed to be peering for a moment in their direction—as though maybe he'd sensed their presence. And this time Doc saw

immediately who it was. It was the toadlike Cristóbal, the one who'd given Doc that horsewhipping
he hadn't forgotten and never would.

Cristóbal, evidently satisfied that he'd been
imagining things, turned to watch the battle
again. Once more, Doc and Joe continued toward
him.

Now that they were nearer, their progress was
even more painfully slow. Each man had to be
careful not to make the slightest sound—a belt
buckle scraping in the dirt might reach Cristóbal's
ears from this distance. Doc put his eyes on the
rifle Cristóbal held across his chest. That was the
immediate prize to be taken; after they had it
they'd figure out what to do next.

In the west, the sun was sinking rapidly. The
sky there was turning a fiery red and sending long
shadows out behind everything in the desert. Near
Spanish Rock, Magrue was bunching his men together now, and Doc noticed that no shots were
coming toward them from the top of the plateau.
Easy enough to guess that the Indians were out of
ammunition—Magrue must have figured on it,
patiently spending the day drawing their fire until
their only effective means of defense was exhausted.

Doc wondered where the hell Raider was. He'd
squinted hard at the rock several times, hoping to
catch sight of him, but had seen no sign of his
partner. He was probably keeping cover, which was
the smart thing to do, and, since he'd had only his
gunbelt and the cartridges in it, chances were he,
too, was out of ammunition by now.

The Indians seemed to be out of arrows, too.
For a while there, they'd been sending the shafts
downward, while Magrue's men kept just out of
their range, so that they didn't do much damage.

Unless they were playing it cozy—waiting for Magrue to charge up those steps and then blasting him and his men with whatever they had left. That was the way Doc would have done it, though he doubted the Indians had had time to work out such a strategy.

Ahead of Doc now, Joe Sunbird had reached the packhorses. He stood up, concealing himself behind one of them. Doc slithered forward a few more feet so that he'd be able to do the same. Joe didn't wait for him. Joe came around the horse's withers fast, sprang at Cristóbal, and plunged his knife, angled slightly upward, into the man's kidney. Cristóbal dropped without a sound. The kidney stab always did it that way, for some reason.

Crouching low, Doc scuttled to where Cristóbal had fallen and looked down upon him. He'd looked like a toad when alive. Now, with his pop eyes staring and quite still, he looked like a dead toad. Joe was leaning over to wipe the blade of his knife on the coarse grass.

"I almost wish you'd saved him for me," said Doc.

"No you don't," said Joe. "You gringos don't like a knife. Don't know how to use one worth a shit, either."

"We can do what we have to, when we have to," Doc muttered routinely. He picked up Cristóbal's fallen rifle, tossed it to Joe, then bent over the dead man to retrieve the .45 out of his holster. Both men then moved behind the packhorses so that none of Magrue's attackers, still some distance ahead at the foot of the rock, would notice them.

Joe busied himself at the saddlebag of the horse that concealed them, one of the riding horses mixed in with the group. A moment later he withdrew a pint bottle of whiskey from it, grinning with the luck of one who has found what he's after the first time. He opened the bottle, swigged, and said, "Ahhh!"

"Now I know why you joined in," said Doc.

"Goddamn right," said Joe. He put a single, quizzical eye on Doc. "Okay, what we supposed to do now?"

"Got an idea," said Doc.

"You always got ideas. Too goddamned many."

Doc ignored that and went on. "First, we take two of these broomtails for ourselves. Then we hoop and holler and drive the rest off. Magrue's men'll see it. They might break off that attack of theirs long enough to come chasin' after their horses."

"Yeah," said Joe laconically. "And chase us, too."

"That's part of it."

Joe tilted the whiskey bottle again. "Maybe catch up with us, hey? Twenty o' them, two of us. No goddamn good."

"Only thing we can do, though," said Doc.

Joe scowled. "How you get me into all this?"

"You gonna do it or not?"

"I piss in your mother's milk," Joe grumbled.

"Shut up, and let's move," said Doc.

CHAPTER SIXTEEN

The torch filled the underground cubicle with an eerie, flickering light and with a choking odor of smoke and burning coal oil, relieved only slightly by the draft that came from the passageway. Several of Tabaydeh's councilmen stood behind him as Raider, beside him, pointed to the small, ancient cannon that lay on the floor. Professor Ashley was on the other side of the chief, staring around the room in wonder. Kara was back a step or two, her dark, almond-shaped eyes large and a little frightened, but the rest of her delicate visage impassive.

"That's the baby," Raider said, touching the cannon with his toe. It was perhaps the length of a long rifle, with the decorative scrolls inscribed upon it still visible through the green patina that had formed on the bronze over the centuries.

"A falconet!" said the professor. "They were used on ships as stern pieces, but could be adapted for small land vehicles, as this one has been. Made to throw a one-pound ball."

"Figured you'd know," said Raider.

Tabaydeh spoke, gesturing, and Kara translated. "Tabaydeh understands about the cannon—but he says there's no ammunition for it."

"The hell there ain't," said Raider. "First, there's all that powder—where you and I went, Kara. Second, there's all those arrowheads."

"Arrowheads?"

"All over the place, in baskets. The ones the old men use to put on the shafts, like that's all they got to do all day."

196

When Kara passed this much on to the chief, he nodded, grasping Raider's plan immediately. He spoke sharply to his men, who came forward to lift the two hundred-fifty pound weapon and carry it from the room.

Minutes later everyone was at the rim of the plateau where the trail of steps cut into the rock reached the summit. Indians, scurrying about in haste, had been carrying out the chief's orders. A keg of powder had been brought to the site, opened, and stirred to mix in the ingredients that had settled over a period of time. Other Indians had busied themselves constructing a mounting of thick poles, lashed together, for the cannon. Women were squatting to one side, tearing off squares of cloth to be used for wadding. One old man, working quickly and skillfully, had put together a ramrod out of a smaller pole and a patch of buckskin stuffed with raw wool sheared from one of their sheep. At the very edge of the rim, defenders continued to watch Magrue and his men below, while those making these preparations stayed back a few yards, out of sight. The lowering sun threw its reddish light over everything, and the purple shadows lengthened as though to reach out for the coming darkness.

Raider glanced at Professor Ashley, who had donned his linen duster and fore-and-aft cap again, and who was hovering at the edges of all this activity like some pilgrim who had wandered to another world to see sights he'd always dreamed of seeing. He was blinking at all of it with his mild gray eyes, unaware, as far as Raider knew, that the defenders atop the rock were by no means out of the pickle barrel yet. Well, Raider figured to himself with an inward sigh, that was one way to keep from worrying—ignore the danger by putting your thoughts somewhere else. It saved wear and tear on a man's gut feelings, but it sure didn't get much done.

"Professor—"

"Yes, Mr. Raider?"

"I don't suppose you know how much powder these things are supposed to get, do you?"

"As a matter of fact, I do," said Ashley. "Half the weight of the shot was the rule of thumb. And since this is a one-pounder—"

"Okay, I got it. We can figure a half pound by heft. I've watched soldiers use these things, so I got a rough idea, anyway. Next thing we need's a tub of water to swab it out each time."

"Not water," said the professor.

"What do you mean, not water?"

Ashley looked faintly embarrassed. "The residue needs to be cleaned out properly, as I understand it. I've read about it many times in the old accounts. Not water. Uh, urine."

Raider stared at him for a moment before he realized he was quite serious. Then he turned toward Kara and the chief again. "That's how we do it, then," he said, shrugging. "Get a tub. Line everybody up."

Warriors at the edge of the rock were chattering and gesturing toward the chief. He trotted in that direction to take a look, Raider following. There was still enough light so that the attackers below could be seen, and, swinging his eyes across the flat, Raider saw that about half of Magrue's force had broken off from the siege to run toward the spot where they'd left their horses. Beyond that area, two riders were going off at a full gallop, sending up a feathering trail of dust behind them.

"Now what in hell's goin' on?" Raider asked himself, and anyone else who might be listening.

Tabaydeh was peering intently through the network of wrinkles that converged upon his eyes. He spoke softly, and Kara translated. "One of those two men is Joe Sunbird. The other is some white man he's never seen before."

Raider's eyebrows rose. "He can make 'em out that far off?"

"Of course," said Kara.

"It's gotta be Doc, ridin' with Joe. They're drawin' 'em off for us. Half of 'em, anyway."

By this time the pursuers had reached the horses, which had been untethered and scattered; they were chasing after them in several directions, each man desperately trying to find a mount for himself.

Watching, Raider assessed the situation. "Magrue maybe won't be so quick to come chargin' up with only half his men," he said reflectively. "That gives us some time, anyway. Come on. Let's get back to settin' up that cannon."

Doc and Joe were riding hard, glancing back occasionally to see how much, if any, their pursuers were gaining on them. Skillfully holding his balance in the saddle, Joe lifted the pint bottle to his lips at intervals and swigged from it. The men chasing them were a good half-mile behind, but they should have been farther off than that, considering the head start. Doc thought he knew why they were gaining: He and Joe had grabbed the handiest horses, and, without time to examine the animals carefully, they'd chosen two of the sorriest steeds, one a hook-nosed, painted Indian pony, the other a yellow mare that must have been some colt's grandmother.

"Keep goin'!" Doc called to Joe. "Soon as it's dark we oughta shake 'em!"

Joe grunted and took another drink.

It was deep twilight now, with the sun below the line of the continental divide, far to the west. The first stars were appearing to the east, to start blinking at the night, and the edge of a three-quarter moon was nosing up over the horizon in that direction.

Doc was hungry. Powerful hungry. He hadn't had a meal since he'd escaped from the cell in Tesqua, and he was cussing himself now for not grabbing some food from the packhorses when he and Joe had been next to them. He knew also that all he'd been through—the plunge into the gorge, the climb out of it, and then his stumbling walk through the blazing sunshine before Joe had come along—had weakened him considerably. He was having all he could do to stay in the saddle. Couldn't fall now, though. Couldn't let those bastards behind them get to him. They'd remove him from the landscape permanently for sure this time, and, that done, they'd go back and get Raider. Doc hadn't stopped them from getting up that cliffside and taking the village; he'd just put it off awhile, and he wasn't so sure now that had done one damned bit of good.

And if all that happened, it would mean that he and Raider had failed in their mission for the first time. Not that he gave a damn what the Pinkerton brothers would think about that; it was his own pride that had a burr in it. Which was kind of stupid when you thought it over. Pride didn't buy fine pipe tobacco and well-rounded women. For that matter, neither did the insulting wages the Pinkertons paid them. He didn't know why he'd stuck with it all this time. He'd had plenty of chances to do something else, and if he'd had the good sense to take them he wouldn't be up to his ass in alligators now, the way he was.

If he and Raider got out of this one—by some damn miracle—Doc told himself, he'd put it up to his partner for both of them to leave the agency once and for all. Or, if Raider didn't want to, Doc might just split away on his own. He might even take up the offer Genevieve seemed to be making with those hints of hers she tossed at him once in a while. Go back east, marry up with her. Live in some house somewhere on an elm-shaded street and raise a herd of squawling brats. But no—he guessed he wouldn't want that. Be nice, though, if Genevieve couldn't have kids, the way it was with some women. Those oversize melons and that big, rounded ass of hers would be great to come home to every night and have all for his own.

Had Raider got into her by now? The sonofabitch. He must have tried—not much doubt of that. If he'd succeeded it would spoil things somehow; Genevieve would no longer belong to Doc a hundred percent, though he didn't know why he felt that way about it, since nothing would be changed so you could tell. As for the possibility that by now she might be preferring Raider to him, well, he wasn't worried that much about it. Raider had a hell of a cock on him, but nowhere near Doc's finesse, Doc fondly believed.

Foolish thoughts, all of these; he didn't know why he was thinking them. His mind seemed to be coming and going again. Must be his hunger and the way he'd been pushing everything too hard. Couldn't let it get to him, though. Had to stay in the saddle. Had to hang on—

Doc was suddenly in midair. By the time he hit the ground, hard, he realized what had happened. The mangy yellow mare, who was probably half-blind anyway, had stepped in a hole or a gully and tripped herself. She was sprawled on her shoulder a short distance from Doc, rocking to get up again but not making it on account of her foreleg, which was sticking out stiffly.

Joe had been a little ahead of Doc, but now, realizing that Doc had fallen, he reined in sharply and turned his horse. That, Doc told himself, showed how dumb a half-breed he was. Anyone in his right mind would have kept on going, the way those hombres behind were catching up on him. But maybe Doc himself was just as dumb. He'd have done the same for Joe if Joe had fallen.

Joe dismounted and scuttled toward him. "Come on! Get up! Ride behind me, hey?"

Doc got up on one leg, but when he tried the other it wouldn't hold him. A sharp pain went through his knee, which he'd twisted in some way in the fall, and he fell again. He looked up evenly at Joe and said quietly, "Get goin'."

"Dumb gringo," said Joe, leaning over to pick him up by the shoulders.

Doc nodded toward the pursuers. "The two of us won't make it. Save that half-breed ass of yours while you still can."

Joe frowned for a fraction of a second, his eyebrows jiggling the patch over his eye. He let go of Doc and straightened up again; he started to turn toward his horse. Then, abruptly, he turned back again. "Ain't gonna leave you, Doc," he said.

A shot rang out.

Joe jerked backward as though he'd been struck with a swung pole. Several other shots came from the approaching pursuers, none as lucky as the first one, which had caught Joe full in the chest. He looked very surprised. And then he crumpled and fell.

Doc scrambled over to him, dragging his twisted leg. "Joe? Goddamn it, Joe!" he said.

"Need a goddamned drink," Joe whispered.

And then his one good eye became still and staring and he was dead.

Doc rose in wobbly fashion, hoping he could somehow make it to Joe's horse. Hooves clattered, dust rose, and he was suddenly surrounded by the men who had been chasing them.

One was Busby, the fat sheriff. He was grinning like an infant with a new rattle and pointing his .45 at Doc. "Well, if it ain't Weatherbee," he said. "Thought you was dead."

"Not yet," growled Doc.

'Don't make no difference," said Busby. "You're soon gonna be."

With the crook of his fat thumb he pulled back the hammer of the six-shooter.

Now that darkness had fallen, Raider, peering from the top of Spanish Rock, could make out only occasional movement among the men who were still spread out below, a short distance beyond the foot of the plateau. With the moon a little higher and the stars beginning to show, it wasn't entirely dark, and once, with his own gun, which had been returned to him, he drew a bead on a scurrying figure and considered squeezing off at it, then changed his mind. The .45 was fine in close quarters, but not worth a hoot at this distance.

Kara and the chief came up behind Raider. "Everything's ready," she whispered. Raider glanced to one side and saw that the Indians had finished mounting the old Spanish falconet at the head of the steps.

"Guess *we* are," said Raider, "but they ain't." He angled his head toward the valley below.

"What are they waiting for?"

"For the ones chasin' Doc and Joe to get back, I reckon," Raider said. "I doubt they caught 'em. Too much head start."

"Maybe they won't try to get up here until morning."

Raider shook his head. "The dark gives 'em an advantage. They can sneak in closer. And they don't know we haven't got enough lead left to bring down a jackrabbit." He stepped back from the rim and hunkered down, his rump resting on the heels of his boots. "Been thinkin'," he said.

"Yes?" Kara looked at him almost archly, as though to say that for a man of his talents thinking might even be dangerous.

"Can't see too much out there"—he waved vaguely at the valley—"and this might be a good time for Genevieve and the professor to high-tail it out of here. You see, we hope this cannon's gonna keep 'em off when they make their try—but we can't say for sure. It wouldn't go so good for the Ashleys if they made it up here."

"Or you, either."

"I can take care o' myself. And if they get close, you're gonna need me." He patted the six-gun he had returned to its holster. "Anyway, I was thinkin' about that passageway that leads out on the other side of the cliff. Nobody lookin' on that side. In fact, I been kinda wonderin' why you and the chief and everybody here don't slip out that way."

Kara shook her head. "First, we will never leave. This is our place—in our language, 'The Center of the World.' Second, that exit hasn't been used for many years. You saw how high it is on the rock. There are no steps down, and the footholds are difficult to use. One must be very strong and agile."

"Then how *did* anybody ever use it?"

"Ropes. There was a basket once that was raised and lowered."

"Then that's how the professor and Genevieve could get out. Don't need a basket. Just a rope would do it."

Raider chafed with impatience as the gist of this discussion was passed on to the chief, and then as the Ashleys were told of the plan. The upshot was that a long rope was fetched, and the Ashleys were led to the secret exit, but by this time more of the night had passed and the moment when Magrue would make his final charge was nearer—in fact, Raider was wondering what was delaying it.

He did not accompany Genevieve and the professor into the kiva and down the passageway that led to the high opening, staying instead with the falconet at the edge of the plateau. Just before she moved off, Genevieve pressed his hand. "We will never forget you, Raider."

Running his eyes up and down her fulsome figure, Raider said, "I reckon I won't forget you so easy, either."

Her smile flickered. "That, too. But—well, I think you should know."

"Know what?"

"It's Doc I still can't forget. If I hadn't thought I was going to die—"

"Get goin', Jenny," he said, his own lips just on the edge of a sardonic smile. "Talkin' takes time, and that's the one thing we ain't got."

After several of the warriors had taken them off, Raider returned his attention to the valley below. There was enough moon and starlight for him to see that the attackers were grouping themselves perhaps two hundred yards out from the rock, and, after a quick estimation of their numbers, he realized that the detachment that had been chasing after Doc and Joe Sunbird had returned. A campfire was glowing on the low ridge where the horses had been tethered, and he could make out several figures moving about in that vicinity.

About twenty men, spread out in a loose rank, each man a few yards apart, now began to move slowly toward the rock. Nearly all had rifles, which they carried ported across their chests, ready to use.

"This is it," Raider said to Kara and the chief. He found his last stub of a thin, twisted cigar, and, backing off from the edge a bit so the light wouldn't be seen, he thumbed a match and lit it. "Be damned sure everybody holds their fire. Let 'em come. Remember that. Nobody do nothin' till this cannon goes off."

Actually, only minutes passed as Magrue's men, still wary, came to the foot of the rock and began to climb, but they were drawn-out minutes that seemed to cover most of the night. The steps cut into the rock were wide enough so that in most places three men could move abreast; switching back and forth as it did, the natural staircase occasionally afforded cover for the climbers as they rounded pillars and crevices in the face of the cliff.

The head of the attacking column was more than halfway to the summit now. Raider could almost make out the faces of the men leading the way. There was one stretch of steps about a hundred feet below the summit that rose at a shallower angle and that was exposed to a line of fire from the top; when they reached this most of them would be in view, and at a spot where he'd already aimed the falconet.

He glanced at the weapon. The opened keg of powder and two baskets full of flint arrowheads stood beside it, along with the wooden tub that contained the swabbing solution—even the professor had contributed to that, though with obvious embarrassment. A charge of powder, wadding, several handfuls of arrowheads wrapped in cloth, and then more wadding had already been rammed into the barrel. He took the glowing cigar from his mouth, ready to apply it to the touchhole.

And then the moment he'd been waiting for was upon him. Eight or ten of the attackers had moved into the clear space covered by the maw of the small cannon. He gave the target one more quick glance.

He had already started to lean down and put the tip of the cigar to the touchhole when he realized what he had just seen. He looked again, sharply. A familiar figure was at the head of the column. He hadn't been able to make out this man or any of the others clearly until this instant, but now he saw that the person immediately behind him was pointing a revolver at his back, forcing him to lead the way. He was limping somewhat, as though with a sprained ankle or a twisted knee. He had a compact, well-formed figure and, as Raider could barely see now, wore a somewhat fancy pearl-gray vest. It was Doc—and they were using him as a shield.

CHAPTER SEVENTEEN

It was as though lines from countless directions had converged upon a point in time—a tiny point that was something less than the interval of a heartbeat. For Raider, there was a line that brought him to this moment where he could fire the ancient cannon, decimate half their force, and make them withdraw. For old Tabaydeh, watching everything impassively, there was a line that led to the preservation of his village and of his tribe. There. was also a line for Magrue, wherever he was. It brought him to the instant where he might have failed, but now, because Doc was there in front of everybody, would succeed. Raider was chagrined at having underestimated Magrue's canniness—his instinct for covering his bets. Doc's line brought him face-to-face with Raider at last, under circumstances he had not at all anticipated. He was hoping that Raider, up there, could see and recognize him and thus wouldn't let loose a volley. Which wouldn't necessarily save his neck entirely, but would at least preserve it a little longer.

In this fraction of a moment, Doc, looking upward, saw the round hole, much bigger in diameter than any rifle he knew of, looking down at him. There was a soft reflection of moonlight on bronze. Instantly, and in less time than it would have taken for words describing it to pass through his head, Doc grasped the situation. He could think quick when he had to, and had often pirooted Raider for, as Doc firmly believed, being slower in his thoughts. Raised in the streets of a big city, where there was danger around every corner, Doc had learned to think fast in order to survive. Big round hole . . . bronze . . . Spanish artifacts . . . a cannon. Hell, yes, it had to be a cannon!

On the edge of all this, there was something else to think about. Sheriff Busby, panting from the climb, was behind him with a .45 aimed at his spine. He'd herded him forward with glee, poking him painfully with the six-gun several times. Puffing the way he was, Busby wasn't at his sharpest —which wasn't too damned sharp, anyway. So the other two things Doc did, all in that tiny sliver of time, was weigh the odds and devise a plan.

There was no guarantee that it would work, but it seemed worth a try, especially since, if nothing was done, they were goners anyway.

He knew that Busby, behind him, either had not seen the cannon yet or, if he had, hadn't recognized it for what it was. His wits were as fat and sluggish as his body; Magrue hadn't made many mistakes, but sending Busby to lead the way and push Doc along had been one of them. With someone sharper behind him, Doc might have thought twice about trying what he had in mind. And there was no time to think twice. Too much of that fraction of a second had gone by already.

Doc threw himself to one side, knowing he'd go tumbling down the cliff, and not caring, and at the same time he yelled, "Let 'er go, Rade!"

Doc was wrong about Raider. He could think fast, too. When he had to. Seeing Doc's movement before he heard his cry—and this, again, was in a part of a second too small to measure—he had already anticipated what Doc meant to do; his glowing cigar tip was already moving toward the touchhole.

The explosion was immense in the clear stillness

of the night. For a moment a great cloud of dirty white smoke obscured Raider's view of the men on the rock steps below. The small cannon reeled back, tearing at the framework to which the Indians had lashed it, bouncing it back a foot or two. Then, as the smoke thinned away, Raider saw sprawling bodies, others tumbling down the steep slope of the rock, some writhing, some quite motionless. Fat Sheriff Busby was flat on his back, staring at the sky. He couldn't see Doc. He was way the hell down there somewhere; Raider hoped he hadn't killed himself in the fall.

The men behind the group that had taken the cannon blast were already scrambling back down the steps again in confusion. Along the edge of the plateau, the archers were sending the few shafts they'd saved into them. Raider saw several arrows sink deep in men's backs and even their buttocks as they found their marks.

It was hard to count in the dim light, but Raider, scanning the valley floor, reckoned that no more than five of Magrue's men made it all the way down. He saw their running figures heading for the rise where the horses had been left. They were running hard, the fear that was driving them evident in the way they ran.

Chief Tabaydeh raised his ancient rifle and called out something that sounded like *"Holahhh!"* The warriors around him repeated the cry.

Raider was already skipping and stumbling down the winding rock stairway. Behind him, the Indians had begun some sort of chant, and he knew they'd begun to shuffle their feet in a victory dance. At the bottom, Raider circled or stepped over several bodies and, moments later, came upon the figure he'd been looking for. Doc was sprawled hard on his side in a wiry clump of stunted pinyon growth that grew from a cluster of rocks. He looked quite motionless. Raider ran up to him and bent over him.

"Doc?"

Doc opened both eyes, then blinked at Raider. "Got yourself into a goddamn mess, didn't you?" he said, the sound of groaning underlying his words. "Next time you better not send me off so damned quick!"

Genevieve and Professor Ashley had watched the assault on the rock from a hillock nearly a half-mile away and to the northeast. They were standing there now, staring at the spots of light from the moving torches that were beginning to appear along the summit. The descent from the exit on the north face had been uncomfortable, the rope slings around them biting into their chests, but they'd finally hit bottom and, afoot, had made a wide circle away from the rock to avoid being seen by Magrue or any of his men. Somewhat exhausted, they had reached this knoll, and from it they had observed the explosion of the cannon and the rout of the attackers.

Jonathan Ashley had discarded his linen duster for an easier rope descent down the rock, and in his now badly rumpled tweed suit with its English cut he looked out of place on the desert and a little absurd. All through the battle they had watched he had murmured things like "Remarkable! Amazing!"

Genevieve's shirtwaist was in tatters and kept coming open at the front, so that she had to hold it in place to prevent her huge bosoms from emerging. She was chilly in the night air now, shuddering a little.

"I think they've driven them off, Father," she said. "I think we can go back now."

"What? Oh, yes, of course. It appears we won't have to walk all the way back to Tesqua, after all. I must confess I wasn't looking forward to it."

"Well, everything's all right now, and we have Raider to thank for it. You must do something for him when we all get back."

"I suppose so. Though I haven't the faintest idea what."

She smiled a little. "Something he likes. Do you remember that place in Denver when we stopped over? You thought it was some kind of opera house and we started to go in."

"Oh, *that* place," said Ashley. "The plump woman with all the paint and powder on who answered the door. What was her name? Madame Something-or-other. It was very embarrassing. I almost went in."

"What you can do is make arrangements there for Raider to spend the night sometime. I understand he gets to Denver once in a while. He'll appreciate it."

Ashley studied his daughter for a moment. "I thought—I had the idea—that you'd become rather fond of Raider, yourself."

"Well, I like him now, if that's what you mean. But it's Doc I'm really attracted to."

"I see." Ashley, still looking at her, nodded several times. "Perhaps I was wrong then. When the Indians had us in those rooms and you were with Raider, I, uh, thought you two had been up to something. The way you both kept glancing at each other afterward."

"How did you ever get such an idea?" Genevieve hoped her father wouldn't be able to see the slight flushing of her cheeks in the moonlight.

"I suppose," Ashley said hesitantly, "because of what *I* had been doing."

"You?"

He sighed heavily. "Perhaps most fathers don't talk to their daughters like this, but we've always been very close, you and I. That Indian girl, Kara. Sweet little thing. Actually, it was her idea, though I must say I responded to it quite willingly. We both thought we were going to die, you see . . . that there would never be such an experience again, for either of us—"

Genevieve was shaking with laughter. "Father!" she said, chiding him in mock disapproval. "Was it . . . was it pleasant?"

"I've never know anything quite like it before," said Ashley, sighing again.

Her attention was suddenly drawn to several moving objects some distance to their left. It looked like a rider leading a packhorse. "Someone coming," she said.

"Raider, I suppose," said Ashley, peering.

"I don't think it's Raider. He has a different look when he rides."

A moment later alarm rose within her. She recognized the form of the lone rider. Ashley did, too. "Oh, no!" he said, staring. He whirled upon Genevieve. "We'd better conceal ourselves!"

"Too late," said Genevieve. "He sees us."

"Then let's run!"

She shook her head. "He'd catch us. Don't move, Father. Don't say anything. Let me handle this."

Magrue was swiftly upon them. He brought his horses to a halt before them and loomed bulky in the saddle as he looked down upon them. Afoot, he was like a stage actor; mounted, his pose was that of some heroic equestrian statue. He had lost his hat, and his bald head shone softly in the reflected moonlight. He still wore that fringed buckskin jacket with all its beadwork. And his eyes, Genevieve could see, even in the night light, were cold and vitreous. He had a long-barreled .45 pointed at them.

"Thought it might be you two," he said. "How did you get off the rock? Well, never mind—it doesn't matter. I want you to move fast, now. Take the pack off that horse and mount it, both of you."

"Why?" asked Genevieve, keeping her voice even and steady.

"You're riding back with me. Raider'll be coming along, not much doubt of that, and when he does I'll have both of you. He won't dare make a move."

"It's no good, Magrue," she said, shaking her head. "You've lost, and you might as well admit it. You can't go on killing people to cover your tracks. There are too many who know, now."

"Don't tell me what I can do and what I can't!" said Magrue. "Get on that horse—quickly!"

"Magrue, listen. Give yourself up. Do it that way, and things won't be as bad for you. There's going to be a lot of excitement over the artifacts we found—people will forget a lot of what you've done—"

"So you *did* find something, eh? Gold? Jewels? What Don Luis's family records said?"

"They belong to the Indians, Magrue. Though they'll let Father have some of the other things. Stop this nonsense right now and I'll soften what I say when we get back. Do the right thing for once in your life—you might be surprised at the way things work out."

"Get on that horse," said Magrue, quietly, coldly,

"or I'll shoot both of you right now. Without blinking an eye over it."

The moon had crossed a lot of sky before Raider was able to get away from the Zama Pueblo and set out on the desert to look for Genevieve and the professor. Getting Doc to the top of the rock and putting him under the care of Tabaydeh's chief medicine man took much of the time. The shaman was a wiry, sour-faced little man, and at first Raider was reluctant to have him attend to Doc. But, with Kara translating, he learned it wouldn't be rattles and magic pouches and chanting this time—such measures were for more mysterious illnesses, and Doc merely had broken bones and torn ligaments the Indian doctor knew how to heal, maybe better than a lot of white physicians. Doc himself was confident and, after he got some food in him, even cheerful. Just before Raider turned to go, he looked up and said, "One more thing, Rade."

"Yeah? What's that?"

"Genevieve. Did you—well, you know what I mean."

Raider grinned slightly. "Suppose you just keep on guessin'," he said.

And now Raider rode alone in the night silence, heading northeast from the great mesa to intercept the course he knew Ashley and his daughter must have taken if they meant to walk to Tesqua. The cool night wouldn't give them much trouble, but the hot sun the next day would, even though they'd taken some water in the bladderlike leather bottles the Indians used. And they were still tenderfeet, both of them, who might not be able to handle any trouble, all the way from rattlesnakes to thunderstorms and flash floods, that might come along. Raider had been aware of all this when he'd suggested that they fly the coop in the first place, but at that time the possible dangers of the desert had been the lesser of two evils. Now the idea was to bring them back again and, of course, break the good news to them.

He rode at a light trot, which was harder on his butt than a more even-seated gallop would have been, but which would cover ground quickly enough without wearing the horse down. Had it been daytime he would have tried to pick up the Ashleys' trail from where they'd left the rock, but any signs they'd left weren't visible in the semi-darkness. There was enough light, however, so that he could scan the desert almost to the horizon and, with any luck at all, spot whatever might be moving on it.

Setting out from the scene of the battle, Raider had noted with satisfaction that whatever attackers were left after that cannon blast had long since disappeared, making their own way back to Tesqua as best they could. They'd be moving on a line slightly south of any route the Ashleys might take, and it was unlikely they'd see, let alone meet, the professor and his daughter.

He had no idea where Magrue had gone. The agent had taken care not to expose his person in that final assault up the steps, and, as far as Raider was concerned, he was, in that act, only being smart again. Chances were he'd disappear completely, not even showing up in Tesqua, now that he'd been shown up for what he was, and that was okay with Raider, too. With Magrue out of the picture, one way or the other, Raider and Doc could consider their mission accomplished, though the Pinkerton brothers would undoubtedly still find something to grumble about, if only the expenses when they put their vouchers in.

It was almost morning again before Raider saw riders on the desert ahead. He had no watch to tell the time, but from the look of the sky and the darkness on both horizons he judged it to be 3:00 A.M. or thereabouts. As he stared more intently he made these riders out to be on two horses, and it looked like one of the horses was carrying a double load.

He did push his mount into a canter now and larruped toward them. Chances were mighty strong that two of the persons he saw would be the Ashleys, but it was hard to say who the third one might be. Nor could he imagine how they'd managed to pick up a couple of horses, unless the third person had brought them.

The horses ahead remained at a walk, and Raider closed the distance quickly. Within minutes he had answers to his wonderings, and what must have happened fell into place all at once when he recognized Magrue's bulky figure and his bald dome glowing like a soft beacon in the moonlight. And now it was quite clear that Magrue knew he was coming. He'd halted both horses and was standing there, waiting for him.

His Colt drawn, Raider rode up to the group. A lot of other things became clear as he saw, first, that Genevieve and the professor were bound with lariat rope where they sat, and that Magrue, close beside them, held his long-barreled revolver pointed not at Raider but at them.

"That's close enough, Raider," said Magrue.

Raider pulled his mount to a halt. "Okay, Magrue. Don't try what you're tryin'. It just won't work out for you."

"The hell it won't," Magrue said. "The only card

you've got is to let these good folks get cashed in, permanently. You can maybe get a shot off, but as soon as you do, so can I, and at least one of 'em will be dead. And my gamble is you won't let that happen."

"You're right about that, Magrue," said Raider. "But it still ain't gonna do you any good. Even if you got away from here in one piece, and we didn't, you're still finished. Admit that to yourself right now, Magrue, and you'll save yourself a lot more grief than you already got."

"You still don't know me, do you, Raider? I'm *never* finished. I've been in holes before, and if there's anything I've learned it's that there's always a way out of them, no matter how bad it seems. What happened back at Spanish Rock isn't known yet, and once I get back to Tesqua and put some help together again it never will be. But we're wasting time talking about it. You and me both, Raider."

"Not me," said Raider. "I got all night. And then some. Put the gun down, Magrue. It's all you got left to do."

Magrue was maneuvering his horse lightly, to keep the Ashleys partly between himself and Raider, which would prevent Raider from getting a clear shot in if the firing should start. "All right, Raider," he said. "It's a Mexican standoff. You're a pretty good shot, I hear, but then so am I. It could end up with both of us dead, but it doesn't have to. I'll make a deal with you."

"What deal?"

"You take the Ashleys back to Spanish Rock. I go on to Tesqua. That'll save all your hides and give me time to regroup. Frankly, I'll be coming after you again—but you'll have a chance to defend yourselves, which you don't have now. Even-Steven. What could be fairer?"

Raider thought for a long moment, then nodded. "Okay, Magrue, I'll take that deal. Not that I like it much, but it's the Ashleys here I gotta look out for."

"Very well. Drop your gun."

"Not first, Magrue. Not in a rat's ass."

"Both of us, then. Together. When Miss Ashley here says 'Drop.' "

"I don't trust you, Magrue."

"You have to. It's the only game in town."

Raider glanced at Genevieve. "You understand everything?"

"Of course," she answered. "I'll give the signal when you're both ready."

Watching Magrue closely, Raider had never been warier. A nagging instinct told him the man had something up his sleeve, or, barring that, would somehow find a way to cheat on the agreement they'd just made. But unless he was willing to risk the lives of both Genevieve and the professor—to say nothing of his own—he didn't see any procedure beyond what Magrue had suggested. And it was unlikely Magrue would fire at his hostages once the signal had been given; that would be putting his own life on the line.

"Ready?" asked Genevieve.

"Anytime," said Magrue.

Raider nodded.

"Drop!" she said.

Raider, shaving the time as fine as he could, let his own weapon go the instant he saw Magrue's hand relax on that long-barreled six-gun. Both weapons hit the ground almost simultaneously.

Raider, in the next instant, had almost let himself relax, when Magrue—who had readied himself for it—threw himself headfirst down from the saddle and toward the gun he had just dropped. He'd dropped it so that it fell behind the packhorse Genevieve and the professor were sitting on, which gave him the advantage he'd planned upon all along.

Raider also dove from the saddle and toward his own gun—but his movement was a moment later than Magrue's had been. He was on the ground, reaching out, fumbling, when Magrue's shot sounded. Raider fully expected to feel the bullet strike and was almost surprised when it didn't. Maybe Magrue was a good shot, like he'd said, but even Raider himself couldn't have gotten off a certain bull's-eye from the ground that way, with the horse's legs in the way.

Raider had his weapon now. Magrue had the long-barreled Colt lined up and extended for a second try. Raider squeezed off. The .45 bucked in his hand, and Magrue, even though lying supine, jerked backward as though swept away by some giant broom as Raider's shot caught him in the center of his face, right at the bridge of his nose.

There was a moment of stunned silence, and then Genevieve, unable to control herself any longer, began to sob.

After the sumptuous dinner of Spanish cuisine, accompanied by the sweetish wine that neither Raider nor Doc still cared for too much, the Ashleys said good night and went off toward the *casa de huéspedes* in which they were quartered.

Raider and Doc made tracks for the bar and told the bartender to leave the bottle of Millikan's Squirrel Whiskey right where it was, beside their glasses.

"I guess it's all over but the shoutin'," said Doc, tossing one down.

"Yup," said Raider. He glanced at Doc. "Outside o' you lookin' a little beat up, we came through it pretty good."

"Luck," said Doc, shrugging.

"Like hell," said Raider. "It was how we played it, you and me both. Magrue's gone and they're sendin' somebody new, so the government ought to be happy. The Pinkertons ought to be happy, too, that we did the job, but they never are, no matter what happens. Don Luis is gonna be happy the way his people finally got encouraged and are ready to vote some honest officials in. I hear he sent Susanita packin' back to Santa Fe. What the hell, she'll be happier in business for herself again."

"And I guess the professor'll get himself a big reputation with those artifacts and that paper, or whatever the hell it is, he's gonna publish." Doc sighed. "Everybody but us gets somethin' out of it."

"Yup," said Raider.

"You thinkin' what I'm thinkin'?" asked Doc.

"About quittin' the agency?"

Doc nodded. "That's what I was thinkin'."

"I don't know," said Raider, frowning. "I just don't know."

"We can talk about it on the way back," said Doc.

"I guess we can," said Raider. "We always do."

Doc put down one more drink. "I really am beat," he said. "I'm turnin' in."

"Go ahead. I'll have a couple more."

Doc smiled a little. "And a visit to Madame Valdez's place?"

"Depends on what comes up," said Raider dryly. "If anything does."

Waving good night to Raider, Doc left the bar. In the courtyard he fumbled for the key to his own room, which he'd taken for the pleasure of privacy his last night or two in the town.

He entered and, with a match, lit the coal-oil lamp on the marble-topped dresser near the door. He turned, looked at the bed, and saw Genevieve in it. What surprised him was not so much Genevieve's presence as the way she was. Her head, with its pale blond hair flowing loose, and her broad shoulders were propped against two pillows, and her magnificent body, without a stitch upon it, was stretched out along the bed. Her great bosoms were bulbous and upright, and the broad pink nipples on them had already hardened. Her golden pubic hair was an inviting triangle between her long, well-rounded thighs.

"Well!" said Doc. "Didn't expect to see you. Glad I do, though, I gotta admit."

"Come to bed, Doc," she said, smiling. "Tonight I'm going to give you things you never had before."

"That won't be easy," said Doc, grinning. "But it's sure worth a try."

"And afterward," continued Genevieve, "you're coming back east with me. We're going to have each other all the time. Father's agreed to a big wedding, just the way I want it."

Doc frowned. "Don't know about that wedding part," he said.

"You will when I'm through with you," she said. She patted the sheets beside her. "Come on, Doc."

"You better know," he said. "Not that I don't admire you all the way—more'n a lot of gals I've known. But gettin' branded and corralled, well, that's somethin' else again. No point in explaining it, it's just the way I am. So to be honest with you,

Jenny, come the morning, you're still goin' to be headin' one way, and me the other."

Her smile stayed with her for a moment, and then she said, "All right, Doc. If that's all I can get, I'll take it."

Doc reached for his string tie and started to take it off. Things were on the upswing. Especially down there, where it counted.